Beach Money

Beach Money

Preston Pairo

Walker and Company
New York

First published in the United States of America in 1991
by Walker Publishing Company, Inc.
Published simultaneously in Canada by Thomas Allen & Son
Canada, Limited, Markham, Ontario

Library of Congress Cataloging-in-Publication Data

Pairo, Preston
Beach Money / Preston Pairo.
p.   cm.
ISBN 0-8027-5786-3
I. Title.
PS3563.A3129B4   1991
813'.54—dc20   90-23475
CIP

Printed in the United States of America
2 4 6 8 10 9 7 5 3 1

To Joyce Pfister, George Cornmesser,
Eleanor Gnizak, Faith Logan, and
the late Leslie Bond;
when it comes to great teachers,
they don't get any better.

Son, the trouble with
being rich is you get used to
all that money and pretty soon
you got troubles like everyone else.

Beach Money

$\triangledown$

1

"**Y**OU SURE HE'S ALIVE?" Patrolman Oliver steered the flashlight across the motel bed, finding its occupant twisted into mean contortions — legs, arms, and sheets tangled as though victimized by bizarre Chinese torture.

"Boss. Hey, come on. Wake up." Herbie Gonner, the scragglyhaired kid beside the chubby cop, grabbed a bare arm and jostled it.

The sleeper awakened with painful groans, wincing, jerking his head to the side when the light hit his eyes. "What?" was the only word Dallas Henry could manage, speaking it with grouchy authority.

"Cop here wants to talk to you."

"What time is it?"

"Fun time." Herbie smiled, white teeth flashing like those on an alley cat with a belly full of mice.

"Don't bet on it."

"It's two-thirty, boss, come on, upsa-daisy."

"A.M., huh?" Dallas's mouth tasted like stale rum and yesterday's low tide. He tried to sit up, but flopped back down. His right arm reached across the double bed and was surprised to find he was its only occupant. "You pass some girl on your way in?"

Herbie nodded. "She sprinted for the bathroom when I opened the door."

The cop, Oliver, who hadn't noticed any girl, waved his flashlight over the dark motel room as though he were taking inventory with a butterfly net.

There wasn't much to see. Enclosed inside a prison of faux oak paneling, a pair of concave double beds sat beside veneer nightstands so grotesque Dallas always considered it amazing that some company had actually manufactured two of them. Above each plastic headboard was a fluorescent light fixture mottled around white edges with bubbles of scratchy rust.

A ten-year-old color TV, amateurishly wired to cable, sat on a low, debris-cluttered dresser. Folding doors to a double-width closet were open, exposing Dallas Henry's wardrobe, half of which was piled on the floor; the rest clung to hangers by a desperate sleeve or wrinkled pants leg.

As Dallas struggled to free himself from the sheet, the cop considered him as if he were something chased out from behind a trash can.

Dallas's straw-blond hair was rat-tangled from sleep and sex, eyes bloodshot, face unshaven for the better part of a week now. "Turn on a light, would you, Herbie?"

The motel's assistant manager clicked a three-way bulb twice to manage a dim fifty watts.

Even with the standing lamp on, the cop shadowed Dallas's naked body with the flashlight.

"You work theaters or something?"

The cop flicked the flashlight off.

When Dallas managed to get his spine upright, he stood just over six feet. His lean shape had a hunger to it that was softened around the waist by doughnuts, rum, and ice cream sundaes. He'd often told his reflection that a proper regimen of sit-ups might cure the flaw, but there never seemed to be enough time between naps.

Out of bed now, Dallas took it as a good sign that the portly cop hadn't gone for his gun. Whatever this was about, it couldn't be too serious. Then again, you could never be sure with cops. "Lemme take a leak, I'll be right with you."

Making his way to the bathroom, Dallas stumbled through a small kitchenette, passed a moaning refrigerator and Kmart special dinette set.

As he went into the bathroom buck naked, the girl hiding there let out a little squeal. Moonlight shining through the opaque window cast her body in shadows of midnight blue.

"I was looking for them."

The girl had on a pair of his boxer shorts, but nothing else.

Dallas shut the door and quietly slid the latch. "Come on, I need 'em." Gesturing to her bottoms — *his* bottoms.

"No way. Who are those guys?" She was shorter than Dallas remembered. Cuter, though.

"Seventh-Day Adventists. Some new midnight fund-raiser gig. Come on, gimme the shorts." Dallas slipped his finger inside the waistband that hung loosely around her slender hips.

"One guy had on a uniform."

"Yeah, he's the leader." Dallas tickled her, made the girl clutch her sides to keep from laughing. He slid the shorts down her legs and got her to step out of them when he grabbed her ankle and threatened a playful tackle.

"Now what do *I* wear?" she protested, knees slightly bent, arms across her breasts.

"As an attorney, my advice would be to stay just as you are. Why mess with perfection?"

The girl smiled, as though to say, Really, you think so?

Dallas nodded, confirming his opinion. Then, his boxer shorts repossessed, Dallas eased open the bathroom window and pitched himself out.

When his foot landed dead center on a spiky yucca plant, his mild shriek was reflexive.

The girl looked out the window. "You okay?"

Dallas motioned for her to keep quiet, gesturing toward the motel.

"Oh, yeah, the 7-Eleven Venturists—whatever." She shrugged. "You're the one who yelled."

Feigning a slight grimace to induce more sympathy from the girl, Dallas examined his foot in the glow of a streetlight. A thin sliver of blood appeared along his arch. "Cactus bastard."

When the girl said, "Uh-oh," and ducked out of sight behind the window, Dallas looked around, but didn't see the police cruiser until it was too late. He considered running, then saw Rupert Dawson looming behind the wheel.

The chief's massive bulk appeared to have been shoehorned into the car. "Nice night, huh, Dallas?" Dawson coasted alongside where Dallas was propped up on one foot like an injured flamingo.

The cruiser's air-conditioning was on full tilt; with the windows down, vapors of chilled air spilled out into the sticky night. Dawson liked driving around like that. It wasn't especially fuel efficient, but Dawson ran the police department his way, no reason his driving methods should be any different.

"You goin' somewhere, Dallas?" Dawson's face was as big and

round as an award-winning pumpkin—features that could turn from pleasant smile to horrendous scowl in the slice of a knife.

"Just a . . . uh . . . just a walk." Standing there in his boxers, Dallas glanced up toward the moon. "Nice night for it—a walk."

"Even better for a drive." Struggling, like a wedge being driven through a wet log, Dawson leaned over and opened the passenger door; the gesture was his idea of an invitation— actually, an order.

Dallas surrendered. "Mind if I get dressed, first? People see us together—me like this—they might get ideas."

The midtown police station was a converted ranch house that had been moved on a series of flatbeds from its original location near the inlet. The building's previous owner had thought it was a good deal: he'd sold his lot to the amusement park so they could extend their go-cart track, then suckered the city into buying *and moving* the house. What had been a $15,000 investment twenty years ago netted the man a half million. Now he was looking for a dishonest accountant to show him how to hide the proceeds from the IRS.

In its new locale and assignment as one of the resort town's three cop stations, the house looked like the rest of old, precondo high-rise Ocean City: knotty pine walls, bad shag carpet with more ripples than a spring brook, and window air conditioners gasping with rheumatism.

In a bedroom-turned-interrogation room, a forty-year-old mother was screaming at some cop who tried unsuccessfully to quiet her. The cop let the woman throw her wrath at him, swearing she'd sue him for false arrest because no way was her son, Joey, a drunk. Not *her* Joey. Joey was a good boy.

Two doors down the hall, Dallas Henry heard someone puking his guts into the men's room toilet and figured it was probably Joey. *No*, Joey wasn't drunk, must've been some bad oysters. After all, July doesn't have an *R* in it.

Dallas followed Rupert Dawson to the chief's office—what used to be the master bedroom at the building's west end.

Dallas figured with the help of a few more homemade peach cobblers, Dawson wasn't going to fit down the narrow hall. To make it worse, the big man's legs didn't bend well, which meant there was little to absorb the shock of each pile-driving step he took. "Oliver call in yet?" Dawson asked the dispatcher, who was also his niece.

"No, Uncle Rup."

"Probably still waiting for you to come out of the bathroom," he told

4

Dallas, then gestured to one of two curved-back armchairs that faced his desk.

Dallas had on jeans, flip-flops, and a Daytona Beach Spring Break T-shirt he'd retrieved from his office in the Ocean Tides lobby. He watched Dawson's niece retreat down the hall, remembering her from a bikini contest last summer.

"Don't even think about it," Dawson growled. "Nobody in my family's allowed to be seen with lawyers. Even part-time surf lawyers."

"Gives me something to look forward to if I ever get disbarred."

Since the nation's finest furniture makers were yet to design a chair that could comfortably accommodate a 6-foot-5, 375-pound man, Rupert Dawson had a bit of trouble sitting down. The effort winded him, so it didn't seem worth the extra effort to get his legs beneath the desk.

"We got a bit of a situation could use your help." Dawson drew laborious breaths to complete the sentence as he ran a thick hand across his bristle-cut hair. The chief's head was equally proportioned to the rest of his body, which meant that no way in hell was any hat ever going to fit him. Rumor had it that when Dawson was a child, he did have a neck, but that as his skull grew to keep up with his body, the forces of gravity pounded his neck downward until it was completely engulfed by gigantic shoulders. "And if you'd oblige us with a little assistance, we'd appreciate it."

"Uh-huh." Dallas was naturally suspicious. Police had that effect on him in general. Factor in that Ocean City police were resort cops with a basically small-town mentality, backed up by a bench of judges who thought the mere idea of being conservative was pretty damned liberal, and it gave one's liberties cause for concern — if not panic.

Dawson pressed his tongue around his mouth to finagle his dentures into place. "Had a jumper tonight. Kid took a nosedive off a balcony up Condo Row."

"That time of year, Rup. Party hearty. Was probably tightrope walking the railing, balancing a two-liter bottle of wine cooler on his nose."

"Name of the kid's Judson Fitch." Like that was supposed to mean something to Dallas, Dawson waited for a response. He didn't get one. "You're pretty cool for a man who just lost a client. I mean, it's not like you got an office full of business."

"I'm in the *motel* business."

Dawson smiled sarcastically, as if that were some kind of joke — which even Dallas would admit the Ocean Tides tended to be, accommodation-wise. "Judson Fitch, you know," Dawson prompted, "got busted on a drug distribution charge a week or so ago."

Dallas shook his head. "News to me."

"Well, we scraped the kid's wallet out of his pants, wiped off the blood and intestines, found his driver's license, a little pocket money, and *your* business card."

Dallas figured lots of people had his card. He tended to leave them floating around bars, figuring drunks would use them to pick peanuts out of their teeth and call him if they got a DWI. "I guess, what you're saying then is — a little Ocean City logic — since the kid had my card, I know why he jumped. Or do you figure I pushed him over the edge because he didn't pay his retainer?"

Dawson shrugged heavy shoulders like any of that was possible. "Just thought maybe you'd help us out."

Dallas stood, rapped his good-bye on Dawson's desk between two stacks of files. "Next time you want to ruin my night, call first, okay?"

"You sayin' you don't know anything 'bout why this boy might have jumped?"

Out in the hall, his back to the chief, Dallas yelled over the groan of an air-conditioning compressor kicking in. "I don't even know the kid. *Period.*" Thinking, Damn, talk about cops with nothing better to do. Follow a lead as promising as a hard-on in a convent. Wake me up in the middle of the night. Dallas shook his head all the way to the parking lot, then realized he had no wheels to get back to the motel. "Damnit." He hit the highway with his thumb out.

2

"WHY DON'T YOU put on a bathing suit — something small." Dallas smiled at Susan Vette from beneath the brim of a Miami Hurricanes baseball cap. Tilting a canvas beach chair as far back as it would go without toppling him into golden sand, Dallas admired the view of his Ocean Tides day manager.

Susan Vette's slender arms were crossed over a peach-colored blouse. She gave him the pleasant smirk of a schoolteacher rebuffing the come-on of a good-looking student; able to pull it off even though she was thirty-one to Dallas's thirty-five.

Susan had a lean figure that did nice things to clothes; the sort of body that could sell wet grocery bags as high chic. She stood barefoot in the sand, the straps of her low-heeled shoes dangled over one finger.

"Come on, Suz," Dallas urged, ignoring her disapproval. "I'll let you borrow my boogie board. Look. A new one. Dual fins."

A warm gust of summer air blew a curl of Susan's silk black hair near her eyes. "Toys for boys," she said with pleasant mocking.

"*Toys?* Hey, Suz, this is grown-up stuff."

Just then, two blond-headed ten-year-olds in trendy swim trunks raced by, kicking up sand, heading for the ocean with boogie boards held high.

"Your little friends are playing without you."

Dallas tugged down the brim of his hat. He watched the two kids hurdle small waves at the ocean's edge; they plowed into the cool water with abandon, tossing their boogie boards over the next series of waves and swimming after them.

There was a part of Dallas that had never outgrown that age — how large a part he didn't want to admit.

Susan said, "Someone back at the office wants to see you."

Dallas moaned. "It's too nice a day." He pointed at blue surf glimmering under the afternoon sun and moved his hand like the curl of a breaker. "Look at those waves. Nice little tube, cutting at an angle. We get maybe half a dozen days like this all summer."

"She's rather attractive," Susan said.

Dallas took a deep breath. He wished Susan would stop trying to fix him up with other women. When was she going to realize that *she* was the one who was perfect for him?

"Come on. Let's go," she urged, picking his boogie board off the sand. Sometimes it was trying to work for someone with the initiative of a beach bum, but, mostly, it was fun running the motel.

Susan tended to the details while Dallas dealt with generalities. He didn't usually handle any task directly, but was good at finding the right person for the job. And he was lucky. Like happening to find Susan at a weak moment, getting her to abandon a high-paying lawyer job to come on board.

The money would have been nice, but Dallas really wasn't in the mood for a client — not today. Hopefully his outfit would scare off even the most desperate of lawyer shoppers. Besides his green sweat-stained baseball cap, he wore a bright red T-shirt. KILL ALL TOURISTS was scrawled meanly over the wrinkled chest in black iron-on letters. His top clashed like hell with green-and-purple swim trunks, but did coordinate with his red mirrored sunglasses.

Dallas was two steps behind Susan, jogging over the boardwalk in front of a horn-tooting tram loaded with sightseers.

Susan drew a whistle from a weight-lifter type leaning against a phone booth.

"Thinks he likes my legs or yours?" Dallas asked Susan, catching up to her.

"Who?" She hadn't heard the whistler. You live by railroad tracks long enough you stop noticing the train.

The side street put a burn to Dallas's feet, which made the Ocean Tides outdoor shower all the better. Sand rinsed off, Dallas went inside the lobby and squeaked wet footprints on the tile floor.

As if there were a monster lurking in his office, he gingerly turned the knob to the single door behind the Ocean Tides desk. He heard movement in there, papers shuffling, a woman gently clearing her throat. Easing the door open, he saw her.

She stood in front of the solitary chair beside his desk. "Dallas Henry," she began formally, "my name is Teresa Jane Fitch." Once Dallas shifted his boogie board under his arm, she extended her arm for a stiff and proper handshake. It was hard to pin down her age, but that her expression of concern didn't drag creases across her brow or imprint crow's feet beside her eyes had Dallas putting his money on the twenty-eight to thirty-three range.

About her being attractive, though, Susan had lied. Teresa Jane Fitch was too starched to be appealing—to Dallas's way of looking at things anyway. He considered a woman's appeal as an all-over combination of physical beauty and attitude. And while Teresa Jane Fitch maybe had some looks, the attitude was all wrong.

The way she considered Dallas through tortoiseshell glasses perched high on the slim bridge of an Ivy League nose chilled the small room by ten degrees. And the hold the stiff collar of her white blouse had around her throat was tighter than a hangman's noose.

Teresa Jane Fitch's knees held firmly together when she seated herself, covered by the business-world-proper length of her skirt. Keeping her back straight, she leaned forward to pick up a gold pen and sheath of clipped papers she'd set down on the sand-beaten carpet.

"I'd like to talk to you about my brother." She was direct, unemotional as a barnacle, holding that pen as though it could do some real damage to paper. She didn't look like the type to send cheerful notes; if she wrote something, Dallas guessed it would be an interoffice torpedo ready to ream out an underling.

Dallas glanced at the wall clock. Two hours until the tide started coming in. The waves would be breaking closer to shore, making for less of a ride. "Is he in some sort of trouble?" He rested the boogie board against the wall and took off his sunglasses.

"My brother is dead." She announced it with the benevolence of a news broadcaster, almost making it sound like it didn't matter. *"Judson Fitch?"*

"Oh, right." Dallas knew her last name sounded familiar. Her brother was the kid who nosedived Friday night off a condo balcony.

There wasn't much room between his desk and the wall, but Dallas managed to pull back his chair and sit down.

She said, "The police think he killed himself."

"That's what I read in the *Coast Times*. I'm sorry. It's a tragic thing."

He felt awkward saying it. Not that he didn't mean it, just that he was always better at sarcasm than sincerity.

Teresa Jane looked at some notes she had jotted down during a few long-distance phone calls. "They said there wasn't anything suspicious about his death. But they haven't been able to determine what apartment Judson was in when he . . . when it happened." She spoke carefully, as though an improperly phrased thought could alter the past. "So, if there was a note, they haven't found it."

"Suicide notes aren't that typical, really." Dallas thought he'd read that somewhere. He wasn't sure but figured it was about time to say something that made it seem like he knew what he was doing.

Teresa Jane hesitated. "I thought you might know why it happened?"

Bright sunlight shining through opened venetian blinds made Dallas squint. "The bit about my business card in his pocket?" he guessed.

She nodded once, a small downward tilt of her head.

Dallas braced his bare feet against the face of his desk. "I don't know how he got my card, because I didn't know your brother."

"How could he have gotten it unless you gave it to him?"

"How about bad luck?" Dallas brushed sand off the back of his calf. It was early July, but his tan was already dark brown.

"I would hope you're telling me the truth." She looked dead at him with plain, gray eyes that didn't give up much; they reminded Dallas of dull marbles, the kind toy stores used to sell cheap knowing most kids wanted glossy shooters.

"There's nothing to lie about. I mean, I didn't know him. That's all there is to it."

Adjusting the sleeve of her jacket to make sure the same amount of white cuff showed at each wrist, she said, "It's difficult to understand what happened to Judson . . . what circumstances would have caused it."

Dallas wondered why she was so careful not to say *suicide*, as if enunciating the word would be as dangerous as stepping on a land mine. "Psychiatry's not my strong suit."

"Judson had too much to live for. He was a dean's list student. Handsome. A letter athlete in soccer. He had just finished his second year at Stanford and was already being recruited by some very strong West Coast investment firms."

"A world of promise," Dallas admitted, even though he hated soccer and financial advisers. "Which makes it all the harder to accept that he could have pissed it all away."

The phrase made her eyes jump. She shifted uncomfortably. People apparently didn't say *piss* around her very often. "I want to know why my brother died, Mr. Henry." Her neck stiffened. "That's why I contacted one of the company attorneys to see about an investigator here in Ocean City. Coincidentally, they suggested you. They said you'd done work for them in the past and that you were the best." She scanned the office walls as though gauging their closeness. "I guess the business environment around here is even smaller than it looks."

Dallas didn't mind the dig. Face it, she was right: Ocean City was a pretty small town. Even with an in-season population over 200,000, everything was run by a tight-knit band of locals whose power was more deeply entrenched than the pilings of the island's tallest high rise. As a result, intrigue — even the hint of it — tended to be scarce. So did clients.

Every summer since he'd deep-sixed his law practice, Dallas hoped for one good case. He could have done it fulltime and made a decent living, but that would have come too damned close to his definition of work — the ultimate four-letter word.

Besides, he didn't take a case for the money; after all, his expenses were low and his tastes modest. More because it was something interesting to do. And lately, empty wine cooler and rum bottles had been making up the bulk of his trash. Without distraction, it would worsen by September. Because while part of him loved being a beach recluse, part of him was scared to death by it.

The problem was the idea of working for Teresa Jane Fitch. Finding out why her brother decided to off himself didn't have any of the trashy allure that usually got his juices going — like adultery, blackmail, dangerous women, power brokers, scheming criminals . . .

But to keep from going nuts, he'd take the case.

"The freight," Dallas quoted amicably enough, "is two hundred a day with a five-day minimum. Up front."

"Do you have a retainer agreement?" Teresa Jane asked, a woman used to confirming things in writing. Then, seeing him smile, said, "No, I guess not," and wrote out a check.

3

SHE WANTED TO SEE the scene of the incident. And since the money was in Dallas's hand, Teresa Jane Fitch figured that meant he would get started immediately.

Dallas had hoped to ease into it a little more slowly than that. He'd planned on using at least one night just to get used to the idea that he was going to be working again. To keep the shock from killing him.

Now, in the passenger seat of Dallas's silver 280Z, Teresa Jane started to roll down the window, but the handle was missing.

"Been meaning to have that fixed," Dallas apologized. He ran a hand through his tangled head of saltwater-sticky hair. There hadn't been time for a shower.

Teresa Jane appeared uncomfortable. Not that her seat was so terrible, it was more as if she was afraid someone might see her in a two-seater sports car that was one-half rust, one-half mostly working parts. To her credit, she kept her comments to herself.

"Been in Ocean City before?" Dallas asked.

"A long time ago. When I was younger. My family used to come here sometimes, before we moved to New York. Jud's the only one who ever came back."

Her memory didn't seem to carry any of the nostalgia Dallas always felt when returning to a scene of fond personal history. He especially felt that way about places where he'd had fun as a kid — and there had been lots of those. But, hell, he was still having fun, it was just a little more complicated the older he got.

Teresa Jane dabbed her forehead with the back of her hand. "Could you turn on the air-conditioning?"

Glancing over his shoulder to move into the fast lane, Dallas said, "It is on. Full power."

It didn't feel that bad in the car to him; his window was down, semicool air blew sort of off and on through the dash vents. Dallas figured Teresa Jane's problem was the career-woman suit she was wearing; the starched fabric that made a rectangle of her figure may have been fine for an uptown office, but this was the beach.

Seeming to recognize that fact, she unhooked her seat belt and removed the jacket that had already lost some of its crispness. She started to set it in the opened hatchback, but stopped at the sight of empty bottles of suntan oil, a broken flip-flop, gummy wrappers of saltwater taffy, and the sand of numerous summers. Teresa Jane folded her jacket in her lap.

When Dallas stopped for the light at Sixty-fourth Street, she sighed as if it were his fault the light had turned red.

"Used to be an amusement park down there," Dallas the tour guide said, pointing left. "First roller coaster I ever rode on as a kid. Wayne and I yakked all night."

Teresa Jane fanned warm air over her face, her pale cheeks beginning to glisten.

The light turned green and traffic edged forward. The pack of cars in front of Dallas's 280Z rolled along like a moving roadblock, finally up to 40 mph when the light at Seventy-third Street went red.

"Tourists," Dallas mumbled, figuring he'd beat her to the complaint.

But she didn't let out the sigh Dallas felt sure was coming. It was as though she had resigned herself to being uncomfortable, as if the CEO had announced the board meeting would run past dinner. She just made the adjustment to bad news — a real company lady — unbuttoning the mean collar of her blouse and rolling up her sleeves.

Her skin was pale and smooth, almost like that of a ceramic doll — about as far from sun-bronzed tan as possible. In some puritanical way, the fact that Dallas could now see her throat and arms was mildly erotic. Maybe for Teresa Jane Fitch, this was sultry.

"Are you waiting for something?" she asked.

The light was green.

Dallas stomped it to compensate for his distraction. "So, what do you do? For a living?"

"I'm with an investment banking firm. In the stock analysis department."

Whew, Dallas thought, a job so dry a mild breeze could raise dust. "In Baltimore?"

"New York." She made the correction quickly and as if it made a difference.

"But you said you were from Maryland originally?" Sometimes Dallas had a tough time paying attention when it was hot.

"My family moved to New York while I was in high school." She was looking around with a student's eyes, as though she could find clues to her brother's death dotting the shore like buried treasure.

"Whereabouts?" Dallas asked.

"What do you mean?" Where her blouse laid closely against her skin, the lacy contours of her bra became visible. Her jacket had gone a long way to hide the fact that Teresa Jane Fitch had a pretty nice body.

"Where did you live around here? Before New York?"

"Hunt Valley."

Some detective Dallas was. Big-time investment banking lady who could call company lawyers, Dallas should have at least guessed Hunt Valley. "So, your brother was getting in line to be a big-time banker, too?"

She hesitated. "Yes." Her answer lacked conviction.

"Were you close? You and Jud?"

Another hesitation, but another, "Yes," also without much umph.

Thinking he saw the truth, Dallas said, "It's hard to keep in touch once you leave home. I hardly see any of my family anymore. Not that there's much of it to begin with. But everybody gets older, scatters here and there, has lives of their own." Dallas slowed to check out a pair of girls in a Mustang GT in the center lane; they had the top down and were bouncing in the front seat to a pop tune that blared on the radio. Ahh, summer. "For a while—after I first took over the motel—I saw some long-lost third cousins who glided in for freebie weekends. But they only did that once. We're not known for repeat business at the Ocean Tides."

"Holidays," Teresa Jane said, and her voice actually softened some. "That was the only time Judson went home. Even then, he didn't spend much time with the family. It didn't seem like he and I had anything to talk about anymore. When we were kids, even with our age difference, we'd talk for hours. Especially late at night, we'd talk about how we were going to change the world. What grand lives we were going to live. How much fun we'd have. And what we'd . . ." Her voice pinched off, almost as if it was a moral offense to admit things that were so personal to a stranger.

"Hell, it's easy being a kid," Dallas said.

"You think so?"

"Sure. Being a kid's great. Too bad nobody tells you that at the time."

"Maybe." She sounded surprisingly doubtful, but didn't pursue any debate on the matter.

Dallas moved over to the slow lane. They were almost there. "Was your brother down here with friends?"

"I guess. For the last two summers he'd been living here."

"Working? Hanging out?"

She shrugged. "I presume working. Our father isn't much on allowances. We're not trust-fund types." Again — like telling him she worked in New York — she was establishing some sense of pride.

They were in a good run of traffic now, making it through the lights, catching a little more breeze through the single window that had agreed to open.

With her hair being tousled and a few buttons undone, Teresa Jane appeared far more casual, almost beachish. She'd done away with her tortoiseshell glasses in Dallas's office, because once the check had been written there didn't seem to be any other fine-print work. Presumably, the details were now up to Dallas.

He wondered if he should point out that he wasn't big on details. Maybe after her check cleared.

"Do you have an address for your brother?"

"Unfortunately, no. I used to write Judson at a P.O. box. He said that was the easiest way."

Sounded like the usual shoestring Ocean City existence to Dallas: kids moving from place to place, dodging landlords who got fed up with too many beer parties and late rent payments. But it's tough covering your share of a $6,000 seasonal nut on $6 an hour before taxes and food, especially if you tack on car payments, gasoline, and the latest fashions.

Simple mathematics showed that the best way to get by was to cram as many people in an apartment as possible, avoid running the air-conditioning unless it got hotter than ninety, and fix lots of spaghetti and Ragú.

Dallas said, "Did your brother ever show any signs of mental illness? Instability?"

"Not that I know of. No." Teresa Jane was mildly offended, as if he were throwing acid on the roots of her family tree.

"Was he into anything unusual?"

"Like what?"

"I don't know. General weirdness. The stuff that keeps parents up nights."

Teresa Jane actually laughed at that, almost sourly.

Dallas grinned hopefully, feeling like an explorer discovering a new tropical island; until then, he thought maybe she'd been born without a laugh gene. "What's so funny?"

Teresa Jane laid her palms flat against her knees to establish a foundation for her thought. "My father doesn't stay up nights about anything."

"Oh. So what you're saying is your brother was basically a pretty straight kid?"

"I always thought so."

"And everything had been going all right in his life?"

Teresa Jane's gray eyes turned sad with irony. "I guess not."

The Atlantis was a monolithic triangle of gray concrete that jutted from the sand. Balcony walls were poured directly into the structure's heart, making each floor seem like a narrow slit in the building's walls. It was a strong-looking building that angled toward the ocean as though daring nature to lash out with its best shot. But on a sunny, hot day like this one, such strength seemed unnecessary, like naval maneuvers off Bermuda. Hurricanes, hah, no problem.

Halfway into the parking lot, Teresa Jane gasped and clutched the front of her blouse. "Oh, god."

Dallas didn't notice at first, but there it was: a dark bloodstain seeped into the white concrete driveway — an amorphous, even harmless-looking tattoo marking the spot where Judson Fitch had died.

Dallas wasn't a student of aerodynamics, physics, or any other science that would help calculate whether or not a body would drift much from side to side when dropping fifteen or twenty floors. The only reference he had was the knowledge that a golf ball, well hit with a nine iron, when lifted about eighty feet into the air, would move ten to twenty feet in a stiff breeze as it descended toward a postage stamp green. That usually left Dallas in a sand trap, but that was a little white ball in a breeze, not an adult human body, which, Dallas figured from watching cliff divers in Acapulco, went pretty much straight down.

With Teresa Jane voluntarily staying behind in the car, parked in a shady spot, Dallas stood in the middle of the bloodstain and gazed upward. To make it look good, he aimed his right arm along the face of the building, keeping his line of sight straight toward the tip of his finger, adjusting slightly from left to right as though deep in calculation.

On each floor, there were two units that lined up in proximity with the spot on the ground. Two balconies times twenty floors meant there were forty doors to knock on, forty sets of occupants to question. An elusive if not impossible starting point. The sheer mathematics of it were disastrous, part of the reason the police had not yet been able to determine from which balcony Judson Fitch had fallen.

The problem was, Judson died on Friday night. Condos rented from Saturday to Saturday. It was now Monday. Which meant whoever was in a given unit on Friday, could have gone home by now, unless they were the owners or renting for more than a single week.

If that didn't make the probabilities seem hopeless enough, the condo rentals were not handled by the building's owners association. That would have put the names of all renters in a single directory in a single office, and an afternoon's worth of phone calls could narrow the lot.

Instead, the rental task could have been handled by any one of two dozen real estate companies on the island whom an individual owner would trust not to rent his home away from home to pyromaniacal high school seniors during "June Bug" weeks. Or, the owner could have done the renting himself, through newspaper ads, friends, word of mouth, etc.

Going through all that would have been a nice task for the federal government — they could swoop in with a few dozen dark-suited bureaucratic investigators who liked nothing better than shooting burrs up people's asses — but for Dallas there was going to have to be an easier way. He couldn't afford to take too much time on a long shot, not while the trail — if there was a trail — was still warm. That would have to be saved for once all else had failed.

What Dallas was hoping for was one of those old retired-guy security guards. A man with gray hair, keen eyes, and an Orioles baseball cap worn at a rakish angle. Someone who knew everything that happened in his building, from fact to rumor and back again.

What he got instead was a bleached-blond would-have-been-a-lifeguard-if-he-could-swim-better kid in his late teens.

The kid security guard had his black high-tops perched on top of a green metal desk. In a white-paneled security office, he had a picture-window view of the lobby that let him see Dallas coming. "Need a parking permit?" Without taking his feet off the desk, he lazily lowered his copy of *Surf* magazine and slid open the top drawer.

"Nah, I gotta place out by the hydrant."

The guard nodded, as if thinking, Good spot.

Leaning against the doorjamb, Dallas said, "Were you working the other night? When that kid took a dive off the balcony."

"Wasn't working, but I was here. Had one helluva party up on seventeen. A two-kegger. Man—" he laughed—"that place was trashed. I thought the cops'd come to bust it up. But they were askin' about the guy who jumped. Wanted to know if he'd been with us." The kid stuck a finger inside the collar of his golf-styled uniform shirt and gave it a tug. "A few of the dudes went down, you know, the ones having the party, but no one knew him. They said it was a righteous mess, though. Made one guy reconsider how he'd off himself if it ever got bad. He'd said he'd thought about jumping . . . but after seeing that decided no way. Said he was going back to pills. Not as dramatic, but a lot cleaner."

"You know the jumper? Judson Fitch."

"Judson Fitch?" Tapping his foot on the desk, the kid smiled lots of white teeth. "Man, that his name? Name like that on you, you'd wanna jump." The surfer guard laughed, then turned serious, suddenly struck by a thought. "You're no cop, are you?"

Dallas shook his head. "You probably didn't hear anything unusual that night, did you? While you were at the party? No screams or anything?"

"You gotta be kidding. Music was so loud you couldn't hear the guy next to you boof his cookies."

"I sort of figured."

"But you know," the surfer said, "Johnny D was out on the balcony. He was with some girl. Trying to put it to her, you know. He might've heard 'cause there was no one else out there but him and the girl."

"Johnny D?"

"Yeah, he surfs Forty-fifth Street."

"What's he look like?"

"Uh, let's see . . . military sort of buzz haircut, wears bright red baggies all the time. Check Forty-fifth Street, he'll be there. Just ask for Johnny D, everybody knows him."

Heading back to the car, Dallas began to wonder what would make someone kill himself. It was a scary goddamned thought that life could get so bad you'd want to end it. Or maybe your head would be so screwed up, it would be like a typhoon going around in there. Vicious thoughts that would have you looking at yourself in the mirror, feeling that life was so hopeless, so tragic, it was worth gambling what was on the other side.

Dallas didn't like thinking about stuff like that. But he did, all too often. For some reason, sunsets induced that frame of mind. He'd sit with a planter's punch, watch sea gulls swoop over a golden bay, and reconsider life's abstractions. Nothing too philosophical or refined in an intellectual sort of way, just the blue-collar basics, the kind of stuff to which there were no pat answers.

Like: If there had been a beginning of time, what happened before time began? If there is an end to space, what's beyond the end? If you didn't have any sense of what was happening to you before you were born, what was to say you'd feel anything once you were dead? That one shot shivers up his spine. The big question. The one that Judson Fitch would have faced like a charging freight train if he'd purposefully stood on that balcony, looked over the edge, and jumped.

Back at the Ocean Tides, Dallas dropped Teresa Jane Fitch at her car, a very sweet Lexus with numerous door dings from malicious New York City parking attendants.

She was rattled from having seen the spot where her brother had died; it was a bit too real all of a sudden. Dallas sensed that her psyche wasn't built for that. She could probably sustain a 10 percent drop in the stock market without a flinch—had likely slept a fitful seven hours the night after Black Monday—but this was different. This wasn't financial fiction strung across a market ticker. This was much more basic.

"Will you call me," she asked, "when you get started again in the morning?"

"I doubt it," Dallas said. "I don't get up until noon."

4

"THE KID HAD an attitude, Dallas, I'll tell you that. A-one-kiss-my-ass attitude problem." Paul Harper leaned against the front bumper of his police cruiser, arms crossed over the front of his uniform shirt. His short fingers were tucked in his armpit, pulling blue fabric so that the sergeant's stripes on his sleeve twisted slightly.

Harper was the cop who'd arrested Judson Fitch for small-time marijuana possession four days before Judson's death. It was a detail Dallas had almost forgotten from his late-night conversation with Chief Dawson.

"Kid was very sarcastic about everything. When I cuffed him, I did it like he was a baby, still, he says to me, real sour, why don't I just use a machete, cut his hands off. Then, riding to the station, he starts in on it. Don't I have anything better to do than roust college kids. There must be some real crime out there I can stop. If he was a taxpayer in this state he'd bitch like hell how his law-enforcement dollars were being spent." Harper laughed, being sarcastic now himself. "You believe that? He actually uses the words, 'law-enforcement dollars'? Like this shit-in-the-mouth kid has any idea about the real world except what he's lapped off a silver spoon sittin' in his mamma's lap."

Dallas shrugged. "He's twenty for chrissake, Paul. You know . . ."

"*Was* twenty. Now he's a statistic. If he'd had a better attitude, he might not've jumped. Suicide's the ultimate act of selfishness, you know."

"I thought it was masturbation."

Harper made a smirk, pretending that was funny, when the remark actually irritated him a little. Harper didn't like anyone making light of a situation he took seriously.

The sergeant and Dallas were at the corner of Seventy-third Street and Ocean Highway. It was the evening's first hour of darkness and Harper's third hour of duty.

Traffic on the road was heavy as tourists headed south toward boomtown, where carnival rides and arcades lined the boardwalk with blocks of game stalls, candy stores, and trinket shops in vicious competition for the vacation dollar.

Whenever the light at the intersection turned red, a jumble of loud music blared through opened car windows and pelted the night with a disjointed blend of new pop rock and classics like Led Zeppelin and Pink Floyd.

In a late-model BMW, the car closest to Dallas, The Doors were pumped up full volume in the tape deck. The song was "The End." Five teenage boys with trendy haircuts, wearing Polo shirts, were singing along loudly, throwing their voices artificially deep, reciting lyrics about sons telling their fathers they want to kill them.

Harper grumbled, "Unbelievable. Tell you one thing, counselor, when my little girl hits twelve, I'm moving out of this fucking place before I shoot one of these horny crawdads."

The light turned green and the singing boys sped off in somebody's father's car.

"Like you didn't do that when you were a kid."

Harper took off his cap and wiped his forehead with the back of his arm. "It was different then, you know."

"Sure. You were the one acting up while somebody else had to worry about *their* daughter."

"Not like this. It wasn't like this."

Dallas didn't doubt the sincerity of Harper's statement, just his memory.

Watching traffic pass, Dallas mulled over what Harper had told him so far about Judson Fitch. Standing beside a *USA Today* paper box, he rattled its window handle. "It doesn't really fit then, does it? A kid with that sort of in-your-face attitude killing himself."

Harper put his cap back on with a fine adjustment; his ears appeared to stick out slightly more than normal with short-trimmed hair flat against his scalp. "Once he got busted, he probably had a talk-to with his old man and got his ass chewed out. Maybe the spoiled shit was going to get his summer-vacation rug pulled out from under him."

"Maybe . . ."

"Thought of having to work for the summer might have" — Harper made quotation marks in the air with his fingers — "*bummed him out.*"

Dallas didn't think so, but knew that crossing someone's opinion tended to reduce the amount of information they'd hand out. And he wanted to know how the arrest had gone down.

Harper explained, "I pulled him over on a routine traffic stop. He was pushing the speed limit. Not that far over. Hell, I was just gonna flag him down, give him a warning, when I see the bag of dope on the passenger-side floor. Right in plain view." Harper hit all the legal buzz words in his best courtroom demeanor. So practiced at shifting into that mode when he wanted to be believed it was as reflexive as breathing.

His voice became unassuming, his expression one of choir-loft honesty, making the most of a plain, rounded face. Juries loved cops like Harper; loved him at first sight, because he had a what's-right-is-right air about his mannerisms, like someone who'd hang a dime-store painting of John Wayne over the family room sofa and say grace before every meal.

"What kind of car was he driving?" Dallas asked.

"Real snappy-looking Jaguar. Papa's car, I guess. Titled to Ocean Investments — something like that."

Dallas felt burned. What was that Teresa Jane had said about her and Jud not being trust-fund babies? But maybe that was her idea of poverty: having to put your own gas in a father-financed expensive car.

"Since it wasn't the kid's car, I didn't impound it for forfeiture." Harper made that sound like a big favor. "But, that kid was on easy avenue. Posted his bail in cash. A grand right out of his pocket."

"You're kidding!"

"Eats you up, doesn't it? Kid having pocket change like that."

Dallas didn't like how what he was hearing was in such contrast to Teresa Jane's description of her brother. "How much grass did he have on him?"

"Ounce. Maybe a half, I don't remember exactly."

"You're sure it was grass?"

"It was THC." Harper was offended that Dallas would question him on such a routine matter.

But that wasn't Dallas's concern. If it had turned out to be an herb blend laced with a little PCP, that might tend to explain Judson's high dive — if something that nasty was his drug of choice.

22

"Yeah, it was definitely THC." Harper still wasn't sure Dallas believed him on that point. "I could tell from looking it was better-than-average stuff, too. Had that Jamaican feel to it." Harper acted like a DEA expert, but there was no way in hell to differentiate between types of marijuana with a simple glance. It just sounded more compromising if it was smuggled in from the Caribbean instead of home-grown on some West Virginia farm.

"You run Fitch for priors?"

"Clean." Harper tugged the brim of his cap, still not satisfied with the way it sat on his head.

"I don't guess he said where he got he dope?"

Harper looked at Dallas like, come on, be realistic. "Said it wasn't his. Same old story — actually, not as good." Cap square with his round face, Harper crossed his arms, grabbing his elbows to hold that posture. "He didn't even say it must have been a friend's. Just that it wasn't his and he had no idea how it got there. Unless *I* planted it."

Cops, as a lot, Dallas found, tended to have a little too much of an us-against-them mentality. Especially when it came to their arrest reports, as though those hastily scribbled pages were sacred scrolls that bound the seams of jurisprudence and saved the world from anarchy.

That protective notion evolved from a paranoia over the court system. A cop's worst nightmare was that some innocent notation in an arrest report would trigger a technicality sure to spring yet another guilty defendant. Just like on TV.

In real life, it didn't happen that way. Most judges were prosecutorial minded to a strong enough degree that, in spite of what the Constitution said, proving a defendant's innocence was a good idea for any prudent defense counsel. After all, those folks cloaked in robes with the wooden crab mallets had spouses and children out in society themselves — no sense taking a chance on some whacko crossing the center line and creaming them head-on if they could toss his can behind bars for a while.

But it was the few that got away that kept the cops edgy. Like they needed to bat a thousand to stay on the team. Knowing this, Dallas was surprised when Paul Harper agreed to let him see the arrest report he'd filed on Judson Fitch's marijuana possession.

In the same station house where Dallas had first talked about the kid with Chief Dawson, Harper pulled the file from a green metal cabinet and laid it open across an unoccupied desk.

23

Dallas borrowed a little police department ink, stole a page of memo pad, and wrote down the address Judson had given as his residence. It was a condo in Triton's Trumpet. Very swanky digs for a kid working a summer job.

$$\triangledown$$

5

"**I** JUST SIT THERE?" Herbie asked, looking up from the *Evening Sun* crosswood puzzle. He was half finished, his work being done confidently in pen.

Dallas said, "*And* watch. See if anyone's moving around inside. If lights go on and off. I want to know what time people come and go. What they look like. What they're doing. Get the license tags of their cars and note who's driving." Dallas ran down the items like a shopping list. "Take binoculars and watch from the southern end of the building. The condo the Fitch kid was renting has a wraparound balcony and lots of windows on that side."

"I get busted as a Peeping Tom, I expect you to cover the bail."

"No sweat."

Herbie folded up the newspaper, put on raggedy tennis shoes. "You going to play night manager?" he asked doubtfully.

"Go ahead and close up shop. Put a sign in the window."

Herbie quickly dashed off a note and taped it to the lobby door: BACK IN AN HOUR. "It just doesn't specify *which* hour," he told Dallas as they locked up and walked to the parking lot.

The Ocean Tides was that kind of motel.

Dallas pretended he was working. Wearing washed-out jeans, a faded tennis shirt in serious need of ironing, and Nikes without socks, he straddled a bar stool in Margarita Maggie's and ate up the madness along with some tortilla chips dipped in hot sauce.

The music made it nearly impossible to talk, which left only dancing or grab-assing for entertainment, and that seemed just fine with the hundred or so club hangers who sucked lemon wedges, licked rock salt, and tossed back tequila shooters in whiplash motions.

For not yet being midnight, it was a good in-season crowd. On the dance floor, girls in short skirts and baggy crop tops put back their shoulders and tossed around shoulder-length hair while their bulky boyfriends muscled up to the beat in racer-back tees.

Dallas considered a move on the girl with blond hair at a corner table. She was looking bored, sitting there with her girlfriend, neither of them caring for the half-drunken come-ons of guys who weren't too creative in hiding the fact that all they wanted was a piece — and just for tonight.

From his bar stool, Dallas tried to catch the blonde's eye, see if there was any hope of him going beyond that point. When that didn't work, he paid for whatever the two girls were drinking — something obnoxiously orange and sweet-looking.

The girl he liked had great hair. It was thick, wavy, and sandy blond and long enough to hide the collar of her Hawaiian-print shirt. If she was old enough to be drinking legally, it wasn't by more than a couple days. But even if she was twenty-one, she'd already outlived Judson Fitch.

Dallas knew the waitress from many nights spent resting his elbows on Maggie's Spanish tile bar; he asked how he was doing with the girls.

"The chubby one thinks you need a haircut. The blonde isn't saying."

"You have anything stronger than alcohol in this place?"

The waitress smiled and hurried off to fill her drink orders. People on vacation were fickle tippers. So long as things were going well, they were pretty loose with a buck. Just don't make a guy trying to forget his two kids are going to wake him tomorrow at dawn have to wait for his beer and shooter.

Dallas glanced toward the blonde again, watched the way she gently placed two cocktail straws to her lips, and took easy swallows on the orange yuck he'd bought for her. She smiled at him politely enough when their eyes met, but then looked away.

Dallas sighed. Not exactly a stellar reception. He was contemplating his next move when a distraction near the entrance caught his attention.

He saw the kid who ran the beach stand in front of his motel having a go-round with the bouncer.

Chad was pretending to be exasperated, glaring teenage cocky. He stuck his hands on his hips, then jabbed an angry finger toward the ID card the bouncer was holding up to the light, shaking his head.

Dallas eased off his stool and headed for the door, taking a route that walked him near the blonde.

She was looking less interested by the minute, so Dallas veered off course, went directly to where the bouncer was posted by the door. Dallas mock-punched the big guy's shoulder, "It's okay, Greg, I know this guy. He's no undercover cop."

Chad looked relieved. He was six-two of lanky muscles, wearing jeans and unlaced deck shoes.

The bouncer didn't give in. He had a neck the size of an off-road tire. "You know what college he goes to?" he quizzed Dallas, hiding the face of Chad's ID card.

"Uh . . . let's see, he gets around . . ."

Stepping stealthily to the bouncer's blind side, Chad tried to give Dallas hand signals.

". . . It was the University of Brazil, Rio Grande for a while. . . ."

Chad vigorously shook his head no.

"But then he transferred," Dallas added quickly, wondering what the hell Chad was doing now. He had his hands cuffed around his throat, pretending he was strangling himself.

Dallas thinking, hanging . . . choking, choke, a choke team, Lefty Driessel at the University of Maryland. "And he was at College Park for a—"

Chad waved him off, went back to his throat again.

What the hell? The stranglers. Hey, maybe Boston, the Boston Strangler, "And then, what was the name of the place, had the little quarterback threw the Hail Mary pass to beat the Hurricanes?"

"Not BU," Chad said angrily. "*God!* Don't you get it? I'm turning blue from a lack of oxygen? The *Blue* Hens? Delaware?"

The bouncer sailed Chad's fake ID into the bushes, told Dallas, "Nice try."

Dallas pulled his car keys from his pocket. "Come on, Chad. I'll buy you some coolers. I wasn't having much luck myself."

In line at the 7-Eleven across from Margarita Maggie's, Chad picked up two cute-looking girls. They were probably seventeen. It took him ten seconds. He said, "There's a party at a hotel room about fifty blocks down, you wanna go?"

The girls' eyes lit up. They thought he was cute. Dallas thought he was ballsy for a kid who just got his driver's license in February.

Chad got two more four-packs of Seagrams Wild Berry from the cooler and slid them in with Dallas's order. "Can you loan me ten bucks?" he asked quietly enough so the girls wouldn't hear him. They stood coyly by the magazine rack, *Seventeen* magazine sexy with anticipation. "And take us to the Casa Blanca?"

"Where's your car?"

"I rode up on my bike."

"You rode a *bike* to a bar?"

"It's cool. I'd scouted out a Porsche in the parking lot. Any chick who came out with me, I'd pretend I lost my keys, then would get a little tense about it. She'd feel sorry for me, so when I'd say I needed a walk on the beach . . . hey . . . anything goes."

Dallas was going to have to remember that one.

Their purchase made, coolers in hand, Chad pushed aside the suntan bottles and other beach wreckage in the hatchback of Dallas's 280 and piled in with one of the girls.

The other girl sat up front with Dallas. In the fluorescent glow of the 7-Eleven sign, Dallas could see pimple cover-up in the corner of her nose. She pulled together the unbuttoned front of her blouse so as not to reveal the edges of a bra she really didn't need.

The girl in the back squealed when Chad's hand got a little frisky. Chad said he was just trying to get comfortable. The girl decided it was okay and then, in a not so quiet whisper, said she thought it was neat that Chad's father bought him coolers.

Shifting into reverse, Dallas almost stalled the 280. His father!

$\triangledown$

6

DALLAS AWAKENED SLOWLY and warily, liked a tired bear expecting to have been surrounded by hunters overnight. Or in this case, Teresa Jane Fitch, wondering why he wasn't out on the job yet. In terms of banker's hours, the day was already half over.

Dallas rolled over slowly and tried to loosen what felt like wound rubber bands strangling his spine. The clock read 11:15. He calculated how long he'd been asleep to see if he could justify staying in bed a little longer. But it had been nine hours. Just about right considering he'd done next to nothing yesterday.

Outside his door, little kids were running in the parking lot, banging plastic buckets against the wall as they reached the stairwell.

Dallas grabbed a pair of sweat shorts from the pile on the floor and put them on. He sniffed a T-shirt souvenir from a trip to Aruba five years ago and, once again, confirmed his theory that if you let something that just smelled a little hang in the closet for a while, it became refreshed. He put on the T-shirt, kicked around to find his Nikes, then slipped out the bathroom window in case Teresa Jane was lying in wait or Susan wanted to tell him something needed tending around the hotel.

It was a mistake, what he did next, but he had to know. Walking across the boardwalk, with the hot sun pressing against his back, upping his pulse, and making his mouth dry, Dallas looked at the ocean.

Damn. The waves were great — as good as yesterday.

"Going in?" Chad hollered from his beach stand. He had the two girls from the 7-Eleven last night set up on lounge chairs beside him.

"I got work."

Chad put his arm around the busty little girl in the green bikini, the one he'd been feeling up in Dallas's car. "It's a bitch."

"Anything?" Dallas asked Herbie.

"Nada. Nunca. *Noooo*body."

In the parking lot of Triton's Trumpet, just before a very hot 12:00 noon, Herbie was seated crosswise in the front of his VW Beetle. Leaning against the driver's door, his bare feet stuck out the opened passenger window. He looked like a pack rat after the fallout.

Crumpled on torn vinyl floor mats were discarded wrappers from a pair of microwave burritos still gooey with cheese. Three Big Gulp cups were stacked inside one another, in the most recent of which slivers of ice floated in watered-down Coke. A dog-eared copy of *Discover* magazine stuck to the sweaty back of Herbie's scrawny leg, while on his lap was the current issue of *Scientific American*. Some of that magazine's pages looked fresh, others molested due to Herbie's practice of physically as well as mentally devouring whatever he read.

"You've been here all night?" Dallas verified, perspiring as he leaned against the VW's door.

"I left at three to get something to eat. Was back in fifteen minutes. Then split around six for magazines. Was gone a little longer then, I guess. You wouldn't believe how hard it is to find this baby around here." He held up the *Scientific American*.

Dallas looked at the article Herbie was reading. No graphics, lots of tiny print, and very long words with too many consonants. "Hang here another hour. I'll be back."

"No problem." Herbie went back to his magazine, not seeming to mind that his usually pale face was flushed from the heat, dripping sweat like an old faucet.

"Can you lift up your end?" Dallas grunted, more an order than a question.

"My end *is* up!" Herbie had one end of the sofa, Dallas the other, carrying it up the stairwell.

They were in the southernmost five-story leg of the Triton's Trumpet complex. A hundred yards over Herbie's shoulder, Assawoman Bay glimmered sparkling blue; near a sandbar, a catamaran's sails hung limply in search of a breeze.

"Wait a minute then . . . before my back goes out." Dallas was three steps above Herbie, bending over to keep his grip. He leaned against the iron handrail and saw his pulse beating in his eyes.

Herbie panted, "We should've brought the table."

Dallas glared at him. They'd started this debate back at the Ocean Tides: which piece of furniture to take. Herbie had picked an old kitchen table, but Dallas said, no way. They were supposed to be furniture delivery men, and nobody would *buy* a table that beat up. The sofa was the only thing in good enough shape to pass for new. Dallas grabbed hard on its base. "Let's go."

By the time they reached the fourth floor, Herbie's legs were quivering from exertion.

"Make it look good," Dallas said, "in case someone's watching."

At this point, Herbie didn't care. He was gasping through his mouth and nose, his thin cheeks reddened from strain.

In front of Unit 401, what Judson Fitch had given Paul Harper as his residence, Dallas yelled, "Swing it! Swing it!"

They swung it good, right through the bedroom window.

"Goddamnit!" Dallas swore, trying to look pissed. "Set it down."

They dropped the sofa on the open walkway and Herbie promptly collapsed on it.

Without any witnesses on the floor to see, Dallas pushed out a sharp hunk of broken glass, reached in to unlock the window, slid it open, and crawled inside through cloth vertical shades.

He was in a master bedroom that looked neat enough to be photographed for a decorating magazine. Natural light from the hall and through the slatted shades revealed a king-size bed dressed with an island-print comforter. A bamboo-accent dresser, twin nightstands, and mirror finished the decor in vacation home simplicity.

Dallas hustled to the front door, unlocked it, and helped a barely able Herbie carry in the sofa. "Anybody see us?"

"Couple people down by the pool looked" — Herbie stopped for air — "then went back to sun frying."

"Let's make this quick anyway."

"Yeah, no problem." Still laboring for breath, Herbie headed for the living room, where bright sunlight shone through sliding balcony doors.

Dallas returned to the master bedroom and checked its bathroom. It looked spotless, barely lived in. There weren't any hairs in the shower stall or Jacuzzi — just a fresh bar of soap and Vidal Sassoon shampoo.

31

No globs or urine spots around the toilet rim, no toothpaste dried on the sink, no water marks on the mirror. The medicine cabinet gave up a bottle of Tylenol, a bar of Tone soap still in its box, a slightly used tube of tartar-control Crest, a disposable double-edged razor, and a can of Old Spice shaving cream.

A pair of matching bath and hand towels, hung and folded neatly, were without odor. The only toilet paper was the half roll in the mounted dispenser.

Going back into the bedroom, Dallas got a whiff of something ripe as Herbie opened the balcony doors. A puff of air current pushed through the condo and played with the vertical vanes that hung over the bedroom window.

Dallas checked the right half of the closet and found a light-duty vacuum cleaner and spare bed linens and blankets. In the left side was a full set of men's clothes: standard in-town-for-the-week wardrobe, which included a pricy Marzotti blazer, St. Laurent pleated dress pants, Hugo Boss golf shirts, OP T-shirts, and a range of shorts from old baggies to Banana Republic safari.

In the top dresser drawer were five pairs of Jim Palmer Jockey underwear in a variety of colors, athletic and dress socks, and, in the very back, tucked almost out of sight, a silky woman's nightgown. It was the only feminine article in the whole booty and it was balled around a loaded Smith & Wesson .38. A further look revealed a dozen hollow-point bullets in a lock-top sandwich bag.

"Boss?" In the doorway, Herbie sounded as bad as he looked. "I think we might have to call the cops."

"You're going to stick by that story?"

"It still sounds good to me."

Rupert Dawson and Dallas Henry were seated in Unit 401's living room. Dallas was at one end of the sectional sofa's L-shape, Dawson at the other.

Dallas was glad they weren't on opposite ends of a seesaw, because he'd end up catapulted out to sea.

"You were walking by, saw a broken window, knocked on the door — which was unlocked — "

"And slightly ajar," Dallas reminded him.

"Uh-huh. So you came in and found the body?"

"And *promptly* called you." Actually, it hadn't been that prompt at all. Dallas had first sent Herbie back to the Ocean Tides, then quickly finished his room-to-room, which netted a folder containing Judson Fitch's personal papers—a piece of evidence that Dallas had stashed in the 280 *before* calling Chief Dawson.

"You don't know anything about a sofa down on the ground below the balcony out there?" Dawson pointed outside.

That was something else Dallas and Herbie had done before Dallas dialed 911. Heaved out the sofa.

"What sofa?"

In the bedroom, two paramedics were helping the coroner zip up the body in a bag. The stench was still fairly ripe even with all the doors and windows open and the air-conditioning going full force.

Dallas wasn't any expert, but it looked as if the guy had been dead a few days now. When Herbie had first led him to it, how he'd died wasn't obvious. He was under the double bed in the smallest of the unit's three bedrooms, the view of him, and, in part, the smell of his corpse, being hidden by a dust ruffle.

Dallas had pulled the body out, examined its arms for needle marks, thinking that possibly he'd ODed—mainlining cocaine was popular with thirty-five-year-olds these days. In the process, the dead guy's button-down shirt had opened to reveal a sizable bullet hole dead center in his slender chest.

There was some dried blood around the wound, a little more on the inside of the shirt, but not enough. In fact, there wasn't any blood anywhere. Whoever had killed the guy had done a nice job of cleaning up.

Rupert Dawson stared at Dallas. His eyes seemed submerged inside the bulk of his cheeks and fleshy forehead like a prehistoric turtle turned face first toward the sun. "Friday night, you said you didn't know Judson Fitch." He paused in case Dallas wanted to confess anything. "Now, last night I find out you're asking Paul Harper all kinds of questions about him. Even saw the arrest report from his dope bust." Another pause that Dallas survived by looking confused and disheveled. "Today you're nosing around Fitch's condo."

"What can I say, Rup, you raised my curiosity. You should be thankful to have concerned citizens living in your jurisdiction."

"Somehow I don't think that's it." Dawson's belly bulged so far over the waist of his uniform pants it concealed his belt's struggle to encircle his girth. "Fact is, I got two uniforms chasing down Judge Fitzwater as we speak. We found out a little while ago the Fitch kid rented this place so we're after a warrant to search it."

"Good thing I saved you the trouble then. 'Cause unless your boys know how to caddy, you're outta luck. Tuesday's Fitz's golf day. You interrupt his concentration, make him shank one into the woods, you'll have as much chance of getting that warrant as driving a five-iron three hundred yards into the teeth of a nor'easter."

One of the cops Dawson had brought along with him emerged from the master bedroom holding a pencil through the trigger of the .38. "Looks like the right caliber to have done the trick," he reported like a geologist back from the dig. In his other hand was the baggie of hollow points and the nightgown in which the weapon had been hidden.

"Run ballistics," Dawson said as a matter of course.

"On the negligee, too," Dallas chimed in. He shrugged when Dawson eyeballed him. "She could have had a killer body."

The chief shook his head.

The paramedics had the corpse ready for transport and were heading for the front door when Dawson shouted, "Not in broad goddamned daylight you don't. Ice it up—or whatever you've got to do—but that body doesn't go out of here until the middle of the night." Then, mumbling, "Mayor'd have my ass."

In a resort town, priority number one was tourism. And one sure way to put a damper on a vacation was to advertise the island as having hosted a murder.

7

"HERBIE SAYS YOU TWO are 'on the lamb.' " Susan Vette was wearing the blouse that was Dallas's favorite; made of Italian white silk, with a matching lace collar and cuffs, it was see-through enough to reveal the chemise she wore beneath it. Dallas had dreams about that blouse.

"We are *not* on the lamb. It's more like being in a little bit of a spot."

"So what's in the folder?"

Perspiration stuck Dallas's fingers to the manila file that contained some of Judson's personal papers. "Purloined evidence." He hoped the phone messages on the lobby counter weren't for him. Right now, there was only one person he wanted to talk to. "Heard anything from Pristine Jane today?"

"Did you check her room?"

"No. Where's she staying?"

"Three-oh-one."

"Three-oh-one, where?"

"Here," Susan said, like how dense could he be.

"She has a room here? At the Ocean Tides?"

Susan nodded.

"*This* hotel? *This* Ocean Tides?" Dallas pointed out front. "The place with the antique neon sign that blinks gaudy blue all night long? It doesn't make sense. What's she want to do? Reminisce about dorm days at Tufts, or wherever she learned to act stuck-up? I mean this isn't the Waldorf."

"She said that. She also said the elevators are slow at the Waldorf." Susan looked out to the parking lot where a station wagon circled looking for an empty space. "I guess she wants to be close by."

Dallas groaned.

"I also think she likes you. She was asking all sorts of questions while you were out."

"A business reference, I'm sure. The woman analyzes investments, remember? She's probably more than a little skeptical about hiring me. She thinks I'm small-town."

The station wagon driver started to pull into a spot just wide enough for a motorcycle, then realized he'd be leaving most of his door molding on the Honda next to him, so he pulled out onto the side street to try his luck there.

Susan said, "She reminds me of some of the women I used to work with downtown."

"And why you quit."

"I don't know, Dallas. I miss that energy sometimes."

"I'll buy you a DieHard."

"What?" Susan glanced at him, that dark-eyed flirting look that never meant anything. "You afraid to jump-start me?"

"Shiver me timbers." Dallas pretended to tremble.

They both smiled easily. It was a pleasant game they'd gotten good at.

Susan crossed her arms and leaned a hip against the counter. "Do you ever miss it, Dallas? Working in the city?"

"No." He didn't have any doubts saying it, either. Dallas wasn't some burned-out overachiever who needed a pit stop to cool his engines. He was out of the race for keeps. "Think of the ulcers. Clients who don't do what you tell them. Pigeons in the eaves of the Federal Building shitting on your head."

"They moved federal court."

"Probably not far enough." Dallas didn't know what that meant. What he did know was that he got a hollow feeling in the pit of his stomach whenever Susan talked like this. He hated the thought that she might go back to her former profession: lawyering in the big city. Although to Teresa Jane Fitch, Baltimore would probably be considered the *semibig* city.

Teresa Jane's room was on the top — third — floor of the Ocean Tides, at the farthest end of the L-shaped layout. Dallas's knock on her door was answered with a cool, "Come in." The bolt was unlocked.

Dallas entered into the kitchenette and sniffed deeply of fried bacon and eggs. It was lunchtime, yet the remnants of Teresa Jane's breakfast had apparently just made it to the sink. A wall-mounted air conditioner was on high, blowing noisy, cold air through the efficiency.

Teresa Jane was seated on the sofa wearing an oversize terry-cloth robe. Belted neatly around her waist, the thick fabric covered her except for a small triangle at her throat and from midcalf down to bare feet. Her hair was still damp from the shower and combed straight back. "Do you need something?" she asked without averting her gaze from the TV.

All the trashy stuff on cable and she'd managed to find a dusty talk show. Gray-haired men in Brooks Brothers suits talking trade imbalances and GNP.

"I found out a few things about your brother." He hoped his tone would preview that the news was not especially gleeful.

Teresa Jane picked up the remote control from the lopsided coffee table and flicked off the set. She crossed her legs, careful not to let the robe's hem pull up above her knee. Once her arms were locked across her stomach, she asked what he'd come up with.

Dallas felt a moment's sympathy for her. He wasn't sure how to broach the subject. "Do you know a company called Ocean Investments?"

Teresa Jane appeared to flip through a mental index of knowledge, coming up with an initial blank, or maybe a *need more input*. "What exchange?"

"No." Dallas shook his head. Christ, what exchange? Did she figure if it wasn't listed on some trading board it wasn't worth knowing about. "Maybe a private company. Not even incorporated . . ." He started to add, "If you can imagine that," but left it.

Teresa Jane didn't show any signs of familiarity.

Dallas prodded, "Not something your father is involved in? Or anyone else in your family? Jud, maybe?"

"No — although I couldn't speak for Judson."

"Well . . ." Dallas sat in the vinyl chair pushed back near the balcony door. It was a beautiful day outside, but Teresa Jane had the drapes three-quarters closed, like someone down on the beach might sneak a peak at her in her robe. "Jud was living in a seven-hundred-buck-per-week condo. Nice view of the bay. Driving a Jaguar."

Teresa Jane didn't shrivel at all from Dallas's report. She considered him with a stony lack of emotion.

37

Dallas went on. "Jud was arrested about a week ago carrying a small stash of marijuana. And he posted bail in cash. A grand he just happened to have on him."

That got a reaction. Teresa Jane shook her head tensely, the movement of her head and neck so constricted Dallas wondered if it was entirely voluntary.

"He wouldn't have had that kind of money?" Dallas guessed. "That what you're thinking?"

Her head motions stopped, substituted by Teresa Jane digging her fingers into the waist of the terry-cloth robe.

"You don't think he would — ?"

"Would you excuse me while I make a phone call?"

"Yeah . . . okay." Dallas shrugged and left the room.

Dallas was winded by the run from the third floor down to the lobby, where he huddled over the switchboard and eavesdropped on Teresa Jane's call. He cupped his hand over the headset mouthpiece and tried to keep his breathing to a minimum no matter how lightheaded it made him feel.

On-hold music kept Teresa Jane waiting for a few minutes, then a very gruff man came on the line. It was Teresa Jane's father, whom she addressed semiformally as "Daddy."

Her old man was callous and abrupt; from his voice, Dallas pictured a tall, heavy-set man with a full head of dark hair styled with tonic. Probably wearing a black tailor-made suit with hand-polished wing tips and a club-striped tie. Sitting in a mahogany-paneled office that cost more to decorate than the purchase price of most peoples' homes.

"Daddy" denied knowledge of Ocean Investments. No, he hadn't allowed Judson access to the proceeds of his educational trust. No, he hadn't given "the boy" any other sources of money. And why was she wasting her time looking into what the police had already resolved? It was a "goddamned dissipation" of money and energy, and she should get the hell back to New York, back to her own career, instead of wondering why Judson had ruined his. Making it sound as though Judson had ruined his *career*, not his *life*, by killing himself. Which was one way to look at it — twisted as it may have been.

Dallas wanted to reach through Ma Bell's line and grab the son of a bitch by the scruff of his throat and bang him around a while, because by the time the old fart hung up on Teresa Jane — slamming down the phone — she was trying to conceal that she was crying.

When Dallas knocked lightly on her door, Teresa Jane didn't reply. Not until he persisted, knocking a third time, gently calling her name, did she come to the door.

She didn't open it, just tried to keep her voice even while speaking through the closed slats of glass jalousie insets. Asking what he wanted.

"I'd like to talk to you a little bit," Dallas urged hopefully, his hand on the knob. "Just talk . . . about anything. Maybe take a walk on the beach."

"I don't think so." She paused. "I need to be by myself for a while . . . I'm sorry."

Herbie walked into Dallas's room to see what was making the thumping sound.

Dallas was having a minor fit, stomping from one double bed to the next, slamming a pillow hard against the wall. "Life is not nice sometimes!" Dallas yelled at him. "There are assholes everywhere."

Herbie shrugged. "Everybody's got one."

The mattress half buckled in the middle under Dallas's weight. "It is not" — he slammed the pillow to the wall and grunted — "nice. Not nice at all." He jabbed his elbow hard against the wall and busted a hole as wide as a drinking glass through the paneling, then stared at the mess he'd just made. "Damnit! Now I'm gonna have to fix that."

Herbie wasn't sure what started this. "You get an audit notice from the IRS?"

Dallas pointed accusingly at Herbie. "Teresa Jane's father is one sadistic prick. She's trying to find out why her brother would have killed himself, and the *old man's* verbally butchering her on the phone from his mother-swanking office in New York. It was *his* son, and he sounds like he couldn't give a good goddamned."

Herbie said, "Huh."

Dallas was a sucker for the underdog. Yesterday he saw Teresa Jane as a one-dimensional cold stone. A winner who'd probably win a lot more before it was all said and done. Today, after the fatherly phone call, that impression had changed dramatically.

It pissed him off that her father could have treated her like that. Didn't he know the power a parent had over a kid, regardless of age?

Dallas gave the wall a final halfhearted pillow-thumping, then dropped down off the bed. He bent over and grasped the thighs of his shorts like a winded basketball player catching a blow. "My ass's on the line for looking into this thing, breaking into the kid's condo, finding a corpse, and the old man's telling her to go back to New York."

"Is she going?"

Dallas took a much needed deep breath. "I don't know, she won't talk to me."

"My advice," Herbie said, "is find a way."

Chad was packing up his beach stand for the day, piling rental umbrellas, surf rafts, folding chairs, and boogie boards into a blue storage box built into the underside of the boardwalk.

Shadows from even the lowest of low-rise hotels, like the Ocean Tides, now reached across the sand, moments away from meeting high tide as it crept up the shoreline.

Further down the beach, a middle-aged woman in a one-piece bathing suit feverishly turned pages to get to the end of a Judith Krantz paperback; she was one of a handful of beach goers who hadn't yet been chased inside by the setting sun.

"Need your help," Dallas told Chad as the kid tossed the final umbrella into the box.

"Name it, but be quick. I got a date in half an hour."

"Girl in the green bikini?"

Chad shook his head. "Her mother." Beat. "Psyche. I'm kidding. Yeah, the green bikini." He made a not-so-subtle slurping sound. "Sweet."

With Chad's help, Dallas scratched out six-foot tall letters in the sand. Then Dallas stood in the middle of the message, did attention-getting jumping jacks while Chad persistently threw pebbles at Teresa Jane's balcony door. Finally, she appeared from behind closed drapes.

What she saw was Dallas looking as though he was trying to attempt flight, Aruba T-shirt flapping at his waist as he kicked up sand around letters in the sand that spelled out, WANNA PARTY?

When Chad saw the woman in the bathrobe, he cupped his hands over his mouth and hollered, "It's not too suave, but he's that kind of guy."

$\triangledown$

8

"THEY COULDN'T HAVE BEEN any more different. My father and Judson. And I think that's what hurt him — hurt *them* — the most."

Walking along the shore, Dallas and Teresa Jane stepped over sea gull footprints scratched in firm, wet sand. A warm southerly breeze blew strands of wavy blond hair off Dallas's forehead. His hands were deep in the pockets of baggy shorts.

"My father thinks the day begins at dawn and ends after the market has been closed and analyzed for trends." She sang the words as though giving a pep talk to new employees. "He works twelve-, fifteen-hour days. Or more. And has since he was a young man."

"How old *is* your old man?"

"Sixty-seven. But he doesn't look a day over fifty-five and can beat men twenty years younger in straight sets of tennis."

Dallas believed it. Over the phone, the guy sounded powerful. What he didn't believe was how hard Teresa Jane was going to bat for him after what they'd just been through on the phone, the guy raking her over like he was tenderizing meat.

"The age factor may have been part of it, though — why my father and Judson didn't get along. My father was almost forty when I was born. Almost fifty when Judson arrived. I think that's too late for men to have to deal with children. Their patience is used up by then. At least that's what my mother used to say."

"Your mom still living?"

"Mmm-hmm." Teresa Jane put on the neat-and-tidy smile Dallas perceived as window dressing. She wore pleated khaki slacks and a loose-fitting print top and walked with a self-conscious efficiency, as though being watched to make sure she didn't take too many steps per block to cover the distance. The mold her footprints left in the sand drew a line nearly as straight as a surveyor's sextant, while Dallas was all over the place.

He'd sidetrack to pick up a shell that looked especially aerodynamic, then skip it into the ocean, see if he could catch a breaker on the rise and make a perfect clam shell jump it.

"For a man who loves money so much, though," Teresa Jane continued after a short silence, "my father sees a certain evil to the almighty dollar."

"Yeah. It can buy you a lot of *nasty* things."

"My father thinks most wealthy men are easily ruined. That they lose their incentive. Their drive." She looked at him as though wanting to make sure Dallas understood this. There was a blankness in her brown eyes, as though she was hypnotized by Daddy's rhetoric. "It's why he won't ever retire. He thinks inactivity is a man's downfall. Because so many of his friends have left work and are now doddering around in nursing homes, or being taken to the country for Sunday drives by relatives who don't want to be with them — they're just putting up with an old man's senility for fear of being cut out of the will. My father thinks that's condescending. He wouldn't stand for it."

Dallas picked up a wet shell the size of his palm and rubbed the sandy ridges of its back. Up ahead, the silhouette of carnival rides on the pier rose out of the sandy horizon like a fun town on the plains. Lights to the Ferris wheel glimmered faintly in the pale dusk, turning slowly, dependably; on a Ferris wheel, everyone's a kid.

"My father was afraid for us — Judson and me — like that."

"He didn't want you to be old and senile?"

"No," Teresa Jane corrected, "he didn't want us to be without incentive, which is worse. That's why he didn't fawn over us with money. He wanted us to make it on our own. He'd be there to give a hand, open a few doors, make introductions, but he wanted the work effort — what made the dollars — to be our own doing."

"How did Jud feel about that?"

"It was a point of many arguments. All of which ended the same way. My father played his trump: that a family's money was earned by one generation, increased by the next, and squandered by the third."

"Sounds like third generation's the place to be." Dallas spun the shell toward the surf and it sailed over a breaker, missing the wave. "Unless *your* old man's got a choke hold on the bankbook."

Teresa Jane smiled as though remembering something. "I think my brother would have liked you."

Dallas and Teresa Jane crossed soft sand to reach the boardwalk where it turned from creosote-coated planks to poured concrete.

"Kind of like a circus without rings, isn't it?" Dallas took hold of Teresa Jane's elbow to steer her from the path of a passenger tram coming up behind them.

The sleek-hooded engine car pulled four open-air compartments along like the head of a stiff-jointed snake winding its way through a river of bodies. The tram riders were mostly families and older couples on their way to boomtown for an evening of loud kiddy rides and ten-cent ski ball — mostly, they wore semi-zombiefied expressions, as though what was waiting at the boardwalk's end was an eardrum's divination of hell.

Pedestrian traffic came to a halt as the tram passed and Teresa Jane seemed uncomfortable with so many strange bodies pressing near her.

There were almost too many sights to take in at once.

In line at Fisher's Popcorn, where sweet melted butter and caramel oozed over freshly popped corn, a husband and wife, each going about 300 pounds, wore matching white T-shirts with *His* and *Hers* iron-on decals respectively stretched across their chests.

Teenage girls trying to look sexy wore dresses with low-cut backs that revealed white bra straps. Still, they got horny looks from boys with neatly combed hair and thin gold-plated chains who smelled faintly of Mennen aftershave.

Farther along, a guy who worked construction appeared especially uncomfortable needing both arms to carry a fuzzy pink gorilla he won for his girlfriend by shooting the star out of a target with a BB machine gun.

"Funny thing is," Dallas said, contemplating the crowd, "they think we're as goofy-looking as we think they are."

He and Teresa Jane were no longer able to follow Teresa Jane's straight-line path when people stopped in front of them to watch an Italian man blow glass into a model of the USS *Constellation* the size of a bay window.

Conversation became impossible as they were forced to walk ahead of each other to make any progress. Teresa Jane reached for Dallas's hand to make sure they weren't separated, holding on a little more firmly than necessary when a group of skin heads strutted by in black leather jackets, spiked hair, and wallets hooked to empty belt loops by dog chains.

"How 'bout it, Ace," a hawker hollered to Dallas. "Two baskets wins your choice of prizes for the lady." The guy wore a cashier's vest with dollar bills poking out of the front pocket. He spun a small basketball on his finger while tapping a tightly sprung hoop barely wide enough to accommodate the ball.

Dallas pressed on.

Teresa Jane jumped at the loud thump made by a football player lashing a roundhouse right into a punching bag machine. The soft bag hit a dial that spun wildly, the impact causing the machine to walk half an inch across the arcade entrance. The big hoss raised massive arms in victory, showing off hairy armpits and thick triceps to the boardwalk.

"What are those people waiting in line for?" Teresa Jane asked, looking ahead.

"French fries."

"What?" She didn't think she'd heard him correctly.

"French fries."

"Really?"

"Yup. Thrasher's french fries. It's a part of summer. Part of the ritual. You come to the boardwalk, you eat Thrasher's fries. No summer is complete without it." In an even tighter mass of bodies than before, Dallas tugged her toward the pier. "Come on."

They walked beyond the game stalls, where you could pop balloons with darts or spring a rubber frog into a pool of lily pads to win cheap prizes. Packs of Camel cigarettes were popular rewards among young teenagers.

In the shadow of a roller coaster, the big ride's gears clicked loudly as it drew a car of excited riders up to the first drop.

Teresa Jane looked as if she were in a foreign land. The boardwalk was a long way from Wall Street. The people paying money for these rides wouldn't know stocks and bonds from Chutes and Ladders; those who owned the amusements were too smart to invest in what the stock exchange had to offer.

The water slide was closed for the evening, which thinned out the crowd. Farther on, where Dallas led the way, was a crooked fishing pier that stuck out over the ocean like an old man's finger. Fluorescent pole lamps cast circles of greenish light against the purple twilight.

44

Thirty feet below the wood-beamed walkway small breakers curled onto the shore loudly enough to reduce the amusement park's din to a dull echo. It was like crossing the border this far out on the pier — two separate worlds.

Dallas steered Teresa Jane away from a couple making out against the railing, but the girl passionately huddled there still urged her boyfriend's hand out of her T-shirt.

Dallas looked north, where open beach paralleled the brightly lit boardwalk. People moved along in a steady flow toward boomtown like sap struggling along ruts in tree bark.

"It smells good." Teresa Jane breathed deeply of salt air churned up by the breakers and breeze.

With his elbows on the railing, Dallas watched the dark blue sea. The ocean always looked best this time of day, when the sun was half an hour below the horizon. "You know why sunsets are so beautiful."

There was more sincerity than flippancy in his voice, which seemed to catch Teresa Jane off guard.

Dallas supported his chin on his palm. "It's a way to lessen the blow that another day has passed. . . . And I'm still not rich. . . . And I'm still not famous." Come dusk, he had no secrets.

"Do you want to be?"

He shook his head. "Not anymore. But when I was a kid, I used to stand here and think about it. Used to look right up to that point, where the beach curves out of sight, and dream."

"About being famous?"

"And lots of other stuff nothing ever came of. But we're still here. Me and the ocean." He watched the waves a little longer. Strange, but in some way it seemed as if he was always here. Life would throw around its madness, engulf him with new pleasures and complications, but he'd always come back to the pier, where time seemed to acquire an unreal quality. No matter how hard he tried to reach out and grab a handful of it, the moment always passed like an elusive butterfly.

Teresa Jane watched him with apparent interest.

After a while, Dallas nodded her back toward the chaos of boomtown. "Come on, I'll show you where a gang of kids tried to beat up me and Wayne. It was over twenty years ago, but the place is still there."

Dallas and Teresa Jane dined on rare Alaska Stand cheeseburgers with mustard and onions, a container of salty Thrasher's french fries, and icy root beer in sweating plastic cups.

45

Eating on one of the wooden benches that line the boardwalk like movie seats, Teresa Jane was upset when drops of cheeseburger juice ran down her wrist onto her blouse. But when Dallas tucked an unfolded napkin into the collar of her top, she pulled it away. "It makes me feel like I'm in kindergarten. To hell with the blouse."

She started to loosen up a little, even played three games of ski ball, one of which Dallas let her win even though she only scored 150.

It was going great guns until they stopped at the booth where the big-mouth guy with a microphone and slicked-back hair guessed months of birth, weight, occupation, or age. Teresa Jane hadn't brought her pocketbook, so Dallas fished out the dollar, and let the guy work on Teresa Jane's age.

Mr. Slick guessed thirty-five and Teresa Jane was too stunned to lie. He missed by seven years; she was twenty-eight. For that she won a pink flamingo. Dallas carried it for the silent walk back to the Ocean Tides.

9

JUDSON FITCH HAD MADE a lot of long-distance phone calls to one particular number in Bethany Beach — that fact according to the most recent statement from C&P for the Triton's Trumpet condo. Dallas counted over twenty calls, quite a few were only billed at the three-minute minimum; others lasted an hour or more.

All in all, for one month, it was a hundred bucks worth. That didn't make any sense at all. Bethany was less than ten miles away. The reason it was a toll call was because it crossed the Maryland line into Delaware. Hell, the kid could have taken a cab back and forth twenty times and saved money.

The phone bill was the first thing Dallas pulled from the manila file he'd smuggled out of Jud's condominium before Rupert Dawson and company had arrived. Dallas was going about his inventory as if he were drawing numbers from a hat; he reached blindly into the slightly bulging parcel, surprising himself with whatever he yanked out.

Dallas was on the flat tar-paper roof of the Ocean Tides, seated comfortably on a folding beach chair. There wasn't any railing, so he stayed far enough back from the edge so as not to be taken by a dose of vertigo. A streetlight at the corner provided enough of a glow to read by so long as he squinted and held the smaller print toward the light.

It was a quarter to ten, Tuesday night, and Dallas didn't have any better offers. Teresa Jane was already in her room for the evening. That the Guess-Your-Age-Booth guy had added years to her life had proven a psychological low blow.

Eventually, during their somber beach walk back to the motel, Teresa Jane had rationalized that if she didn't look mature, no one would want to do business with her. Which reminded Dallas of a line from the movie *Diner*: "Fuck mature."

He put the phone bill under his foot to keep the breeze from blowing it away. About to go back into the folder, he realized there hadn't been any long-distance calls to New York on the statement. If Judson and his father had talked during the past month, Pops had made the call, or, more than likely now that Dallas thought about it, the kid called collect.

The next item up for bid was a duplicate copy of the Triton's Trumpet lease. Signed three weeks ago, it showed that Jud had put down a two-grand deposit for a seasonal rental just over twice that much. It prorated out to almost $800 per week.

Another couple pages clipped together appeared to be a handwritten ledger arranged in some sort of code. Across the top were dates at one-week intervals. Down the side were short initials like *EnbrgSt (NYX)*, *RvBkTr (AMX)*, *Gossmr (OTC)*, a list of about ten in all. Numbers filled in the columns and rows to correspond to a particular date and name; generally, the numerical entries were whole numbers followed by fractions no smaller than 1/16.

Seeing as Jud had been busted for drugs, Dallas tried to make the ledger fit a narcotics distribution scheme, but then he mocked himself for being so predetermined about Jud's habits.

The initials NYX, AMX, and OTC were symbols for the various stock exchanges, New York, American, and Over The Counter. Jud had, after all, been a finance major at Stanford, his blood line was banking. His chart was tracking stock prices over a six-month period.

Mostly, the issues Jud had been pricing were winners, some of them big gainers. Maybe it had just been a hobby, but, Dallas thought, wouldn't it be a kick in Jud's old man's teeth if it turned out the kid was making his "pocket change" trading stocks. Dallas hoped so for Teresa Jane's sake. Maybe he finally had some good news for her after all.

Dallas plugged on through the folder, coming up with a form letter from the dean of students, Stanford University, dated mid-June, advising Jud that his application for a leave of absence "in order to broaden his horizons with world travel" had been granted. He could reenroll without a new application anytime within the next three years. Teresa Jane hadn't said anything about that; Dallas wondered if she knew. He filed the paper under his foot.

Next up, things got less procedural. And substantially steamier. There was a handwritten letter penned in clean, flowery letters; it was unsigned, undated, on plain note-size stationery. The edges were curled as though it had been read, studied, numerous times.

Dearest Judson:
Please consider these words with the love and concern with which they are intended. It was never, *never* my intention to hurt you. And I think, I know that you must realize that.
When we began seeing each other, you knew the limits of my affections. You knew that certain things could never be. Yet your persistence, while the result of your undoubting love, can only cause us pain.
This is why we simply cannot continue to see each other. It would only lead, as I mentioned the other night, to something very foolish that we might each well live to regret.

Ow, Dallas thought. Hot stuff. He dug into the folder in search of the envelope that would have been used to send it. And there it was, postmarked locally one week ago. Which meant, given the usual postal delivery schedule, Judson would have received it Thursday, one day before the fall. Suddenly, there was a motive for suicide.

Dallas used his master key to get into an unoccupied room on the third floor. The fluorescent lights mounted above the beds didn't work — no real surprise — so he had to turn on the standing lamp beside the sofa to see what he was doing.

He dialed the number in Bethany Beach listed numerous times on Jud's phone bill. The line rang three times, then a woman answered. She had a clear, pretty voice that seemed to go with the style of penmanship that flowed across the note. But she was older sounding, a classy maturity beyond anyone Jud's age.

"This is Donny Donaldson, East Coast Marketing," Dallas said cheerfully. "Would you be interested in a free trial subscription to *People* magazine?"

"I don't think so, no."

"It's free," Dallas reassured her. "All you have to give me is a name and mailing address and — "

Click.

Unbelievable. She hung up on an offer for free *People* magazines.

Didn't she have any interest in high-quality journalism? Didn't she want to know who Sly Stallone was dating this week?

"Am I in trouble?"

"Should you be?"

Intent on the contents of the manila folder as he walked into the Ocean Tides lobby, Dallas hadn't seen Herbie waving desperate warnings until it was too late. What was even more incredible was that he hadn't seen the reason for Herbie's concern: Chief Rupert Dawson had dropped by for a visit.

Seeing the big cop, Dallas glanced instinctively over his shoulder. Dawson appeared to be alone, without backup. Dawson would know from experience that if he planned to haul Dallas away, he'd need help, because Dallas would run for it.

So, Dallas hoped, maybe it was just a social call. Then thought, *Fat chance*, and amused himself with the bad pun.

"Whatchew got there?" Dawson gestured with his wide nose toward the manila folder. There weren't any chairs in the lobby wide enough to accommodate him, so Dawson remained standing near the door, arms crossed like two fleshy logs across his gut.

"Bills." Dallas shoved his most recent finding back into the file. There had been another seasonal lease Jud had signed, this one for an efficiency in a semidive bay-front building that had converted from motel to condo a few years ago.

Herbie snuck off into Dallas's office, but kept the door open so he could overhear the conversation, to see if he should phone a bail bondsman.

"That gun we found in the Fitch kid's condo . . . ? Nice compact thirty-eight . . . ? Still had powder burns inside the barrel, though the outside had been wiped clean. Looks like your boy had been doing some shooting of late. Maybe took care of that guy under the bed."

"Well, the evidence *is* overwhelming."

"The evidence ain't dick." Dawson wasn't a big fan of sarcasm. "But I sure would like to know how come your name — or your ugly face — keeps turnin' up each time there's a development with this Fitch boy. Hell, you're two for two. If the Orioles hit like that, they might win more games."

"Not unless their pitching improves."

Dawson opened the lobby door and spit meanly onto the parking lot. Dallas wasn't sure, but it sounded as if the force of phlegm hitting the ground actually chipped the asphalt. "I thought maybe I'd give you another chance to tell me what you know about this kid. How come your card was in his pocket and how come you're so damned concerned about what's going on."

"I'm not concerned, Rup. I'm just bored."

Dawson stared at him. Dallas didn't look away, but he didn't smile, either; that would have been pushing it. Dallas liked his front teeth, and Dawson had one hell of a punch.

When the Barefoot Sandbagger had been re-sided with pale blue vinyl and trimmed in rose to make the switch from motel to condo, it was like giving an eye tuck to a ninety-year-old. Nice face, no legs.

The investor had made money though. Only the really stupid ones didn't. The old twelve-unit bay-front motel had been bought for $300,000; another $75,000 took care of the face-lift, including repaving the parking lot, installing new bargain-basement carpet, toilets, and one-piece fiberglass tub/shower enclosures. A local painter they called the Wolfman, because of his resemblance to the infamous DJ, had been summoned to give it his best cheat-'em-and-run spray paint job, which, by contract terms, specified that anything that didn't move got painted.

The developer set up a model unit decorated with $25,000 worth of furnishings, and sold all twelve efficiencies over the span of two summer weekends. The prices ranged from $65,000 for first floor near the stairs, to $80,000 for upstairs center. The gross was over $850,000, which, less four percent in real estate commissions (which the developer paid to his wife's corporation), still kept the settlement table net over 800 Gs. The profit found a home in the neighborhood of $400,000. Not to mention that the model furniture ended up as a total write-off on the guy's taxes, while looking pretty damned nice in the Florida room he added onto his house overlooking the St. Martin's River.

Barefoot Sandbagger 2-E was the efficiency condo Judson Fitch had signed up for way back in January, which was when most kids came down to book a place for the summer season. The terms of the Barefoot Sandbagger lease were much more in line with what Dallas would expect of a seasonal employee.

The lease commenced May 15 and ran to September 15 for $3,500. That was around $200 per week, which, divided among the three occupants permitted, was one of the bargains of the beach. Two or three kids could work the summer, rent the place, and go back to school in the fall with a great tan, lustful memories, and, if they were lucky, a cured case of crabs and some money in their pockets.

When Dallas turned his 280 up the steep concrete apron into the Sandbagger parking lot, he heard music coming from the second floor. Bob Marley's "Buffalo Soldier" with the bass cranked up. Dallas parked in the loading zone and shut off the engine.

It seemed, from the noise — occasional male-hormone bellows and playful young girl shrieks — that a party was going on in Unit 2-D. Right next to the darkened apartment that had been Jud's.

Dallas went up creaking wood steps two at a time. The toe of his flip-flops scraped up some of the Wolfman's water-base paint, causing dark rose to peel away and reveal the last time someone had done the job right with oil-base green.

Between the music and cheers, a less obvious sound came from the party room. It was the clean, clanking ricochet of quarters being plunked on a hard table, aimed for an empty beer mug. When a coin rattled home in the glass, there were cries of victory, then the chant — unison male and female — "Go, go, go, go, go!" that built in intensity and erupted cheerfully as the round's loser was required to perform some bizarre penalty such as chug-a-lugging a can of cheap beer or losing some clothes.

Dallas tried the door to Judson's rental, which was locked. Maybe he should have brought along Herbie and another sofa. He was about to peek into 2-D, when that unit's door was flung open.

"Fire!"

A bulky blond-haired teenager came running out with an order of Jiffy Pop that had turned to popcorn flambé. Hunks of burning corn dropped through the aluminum container and firebombed the walkway.

"Shit-shit! Fire!" The kid blew on the blaze with frantic puffs of air that only seemed to anger the licks of flame dancing in his face.

"C.J. What's happening?" Dallas greeted him, stomping out some corn bombs with his flip-flop.

C.J. looked away from his bonfire. "Hey, Dallas." The fire picked up in the breeze.

Heavy footsteps, belonging to someone who had to duck to clear the doorway of the party condo, carried a bucket of water outside.

"Jim!" Dallas grinned.

"Hey." Jim sounded and looked tired and pissed off. He dumped the water over C.J.'s head and the Jiffy Pop at the same time. The fire was quickly reduced to a smoldering sizzle.

"Thanks, Jim," C.J. said, soaking wet.

"Dumb high school kid." Jim turned back inside, then came back out freshly incensed. "You made me miss it!" He chased C.J. toward the stairs and threw the bucket after him.

Dallas went inside 2-D.

Having done her twenty-second dance, the cute girl was putting her top back on, having lost the final round of Strip Quarters.

The gang numbered ten in all, including C.J. and Jim, and was six to four, boys to girls. Dallas recognized about half of them, checking out faces as they searched among discarded clothes to redress for the next game.

It took some doing to stack that many bodies in the small room with all the space taken up by crushed beer cans, melting buckets of ice, and crushed pretzel bags. A card table in the center of the room acted as the playing surface. The twin and double beds scattered with sheets that hadn't seen a laundromat for weeks were pushed against the wall.

"Pull up a chair," C.J. invited, even though there were no chairs.

Dallas had no idea what they'd done with them. Everyone was kneeling or standing — depending on degrees of sobriety — around the table.

"I was looking for the guy next door," Dallas said over the music. "Jud Fitch. You know him? Anybody know him?"

They were all too interested in the game. New rules were being discussed loudly. First one to land a quarter in the beer glass got to name the person who had to take the next turn, and if that person missed, they stripped, or if they hit one, they could pass to the person on their left or try again; if they hit a second one in a row, the original challenger had to strip, but if they missed the second one, they had to strip and then pass it to the left.

Everyone was too drunk to get it, which resulted in many arguments and rule changes as quarters were shot wildly toward the mug, and an ultimate appeal was made to Dallas to act as judge.

A veteran of such escapades, but from many years earlier, Dallas joined in at the table and last recollected, around sunrise, how strangely warm beer tasted with burned Jiffy Pop.

10

THREE PEOPLE WERE ASLEEP on the twin bed, bodies twisted to form a snoring daisy chain. Dallas recognized Jim's feet sticking out; at size sixteen, with big toes the size of a hand maul, they were tough to miss.

When someone opened the curtains, there was a collective groan as painful sunlight burned into the room. The curtains was reclosed. The party was slowly, torturously coming back to life.

Dallas's tongue had Coors Light footprints all over it as he struggled to his feet and hugged the wall for support. Two girls were sleeping back to back on the kitchenette floor that remained wet with spilled beer; each wore a white T-shirt and bikini briefs that glowed cleanly in the dim light. Careful not to step on them, and not having an easy time of it, Dallas made his way to the bathroom.

The door was closed, but not locked, which according to standard protocol in crowded accommodations meant someone was in there, but wouldn't object to company. Dallas opened the door as a lithe blonde turned on the shower and stepped into the tub.

"Morning," she greeted him, sleepy awake, sliding closed the white vinyl curtain, not seeming to mind that Dallas had seen her naked.

Dallas smiled in reply even though she couldn't see him with the curtain drawn. About to tend to his business, he was surprised to find that he was only wearing his Jockey briefs. He didn't remember having joined in the game. Oh, well . . .

"What's your name?" the girl asked from inside the shower. Water ricocheting off her shoulders splashed Dallas warmly.

"Dallas."

"That's a neat name. Mine's Terry. We didn't get a chance to talk last night."

"Did anyone?" Dallas was having a hard time firing up the personal plumbing this morning. The touch of excitement from seeing the girl naked was kinking flow a little.

"This your place?" Terry asked.

"What?" Dallas heard her question, but was too busy thinking how cute her butt had looked to come up with any other response. She was probably a little older than the rest of the gang — maybe twenty-three — and a little hotter, too.

"The apartment? Is it yours?"

"I think it's C.J.'s"

"Which one's he?"

God she had a lot of questions. Dallas tried doing a little hop on one leg to get some action, which, with some effort began to work. Ahh, relief.

Then the girl stuck her head out of the shower, looked right at him — and not his eyes. "Peek-a-boo." She smiled, then disappeared behind the curtain.

I love this town, Dallas thought.

"I can't eat these for breakfast." Terry inspected a box taken from the kitchen cabinets. She spoke quietly so as not to add further pain to anyone's hangover.

"Pop-Tarts are good for you." Dallas had a blueberry one with drippy icing.

"They're moldy."

"Penicillin's good for what ails you."

"I'm careful," Terry replied snappily. "I don't need penicillin."

Dallas shrugged. He'd found his pants, but was without his shirt; he guessed that was somewhere in the tumble of blankets, sheets, and bodies twisted around on the double bed. Dallas and Terry were the only two who'd managed to awaken past the grumbling, looking-for-something-to-put-over-their-head stage.

"Would you buy me breakfast?" Terry asked.

Dallas picked a Bad Dog Goes Surfing T-shirt off the floor and put it on. "Sure." He took his Pop-Tart with him.

"I heard you ask about Jud Fitch last night."

Dallas put a forkful of pancakes in his mouth. "You knew him?"

"Yeah. I have the apartment beneath his."

"You know he's dead."

Terry nodded. Her expression was one of acceptance. "It was terrible. You know, I've been around plenty of people who do drugs, but it still surprises me sometimes to find out how heavily someone's into them." Terry considered a piece of toast. She was a careful eater, giving everything the once-over before taking a bite. "You don't expect it of some people. I mean someone like Jud. The burners you can spot a mile away. But Jud put on a good act."

"Like how?"

"For as much as he must have been using, he wasn't burnt around the edges. Didn't always talk about getting high, or how wasted he'd been the night before. The burners like to announce it, give you a running commentary on what they've done."

Dallas and Terry were in the General's Kitchen on Seventy-third Street. It was Dallas's favorite breakfast spot. The pancakes were good, the creamed chipped beef even better, and Gus put on a good show yelling at the waitresses. It was already 1:30, so most of the breakfast crowd had gone.

Seated by the window, Terry used the edge of her fork to skillfully cut the soft white away from the yolk of an over-medium egg. She handled it with the delicate touch of a heart surgeon. "When I met Jud last January, he didn't say anything about drugs or drinking all weekend. We happened to be in the rental office at the same time, looking for a summer place. He asked me out, and we had a pretty good time. Freezing cold, but it was fun. There was hardly anyone in the movies, and we buzzed up and down the highway afterward, running red lights. No one was there to care."

"Jud didn't do any stuff that weekend?"

"No." Terry dashed about a teaspoon of salt on her egg white, folded it onto the tip of her fork, and ate it all in one bite. "But some guys are like that until you get to know them. I guess maybe he thought he might scare me away if I thought he was a coker."

"He did a lot of cocaine?" Dallas went back to his pancakes.

"Jud had an indulgent personality, so, yeah, it was probably a lot."

"Why 'probably'? He was either doing a lot of coke or he wasn't."

A man in a golf hat being seated two tables away nodded his friend toward Terry, told him to check out how her crop top left a lot of tanned stomach exposed; and that if someone came in and held the place up, they'd get a free show with Terry's arms above her head.

"Well, I never actually saw him doing any drugs. But I don't know if anyone did. Jud was real careful like that."

"How do you mean? That he didn't want to get caught?"

"I'm not sure how to put it exactly." Terry painstakingly popped a square of jelly from a prewrapped container and began to methodically spread it across a triangle of pale toast. "Lately, there were times he would really act like a big shot, being around drugs and all that money. Then other times he didn't want people to know anything about it. Does that make sense?"

"Uhh, no."

"Most people do coke for the thrill it gives them, right?"

"Yeah . . . ?" Going to town on his pancakes, Dallas tried to see where she was headed with this.

"They use coke for that sense of feeling indestructible and immortal. But Jud was into it for the power. He thought people looked up to him because he had a source. It made him a celebrity. He was admired — or so he thought. And he loved the attention selling coke got him, but then when it seemed like the only reason he was getting attention was the drugs, he played it down."

Terry continued spreading jelly over her toast, precisely covering every crumb. "It's like Jud had a secret he shouldn't tell anyone, but he was always telling it because it was too good a secret to keep." She finally took a bite of toast — one bite and put it down. "Like his car. The Jaguar? Jud started driving it and couldn't stop. But when he rented another condo, a nice one on the bay at Triton's Trumpet, he only told a few of us about it, then denied it later on. Like it was something he wasn't supposed to have talked about in the first place. I was never there, but I heard it had a real nice Jacuzzi. That's probably why Jud rented it. He had a real thing for Jacuzzis."

Terry's blunt-cut bangs hung at an angle over sun-bleached eyebrows. "How come you want to know all this anyway?"

Dallas wasn't sure what to tell her. He usually relied on an ad-lib instead of planning stories out in advance, which sometimes left him blank. "I'm curious how he died."

She seemed to accept that. "Got a little coked up, it messed with his head, and he jumped." Terry said that simply enough, so acquiescent that life could be that way it was scary.

His pancakes now finished, Dallas stuck a finger into leftover syrup and licked it. "Coke and suicide aren't your usual mixers."

"I didn't say the jump was on purpose. He might've been riding a nice little surge of coke power, hopped up on that balcony railing, beat his chest, howling at the moon like he owned it."

"But you don't know for sure he was doing drugs."

"Some things you know," she replied confidently.

Maybe. Dallas tried to evaluate the source. Terry wasn't a flake, but she was definitely a little bit of a beachhead—that phase of life when too much sun and irresponsibility skews the way logic synapses fire. It's a temporary phase, quickly corrected by the onset of cool weather, or the *second* week of college classes, whichever horror comes first.

"Did Jud ever talk about killing himself?"

"Never. Jud mainly talked about, let's see, I'd say . . ." she counted to herself, "three things. Money. Sex. And what a prick his father was."

"What about girlfriends? Was there anyone he was serious with?"

"Jud?" Like was he kidding? "Jud was interested in quantity. He was very score-oriented. You know what I mean? How *many* girls he could make it with. How *much* money someone had. It was his obsession. He liked to compare totals with his friends, and liked to be the leader."

"So he had lots of girlfriends?"

"Too many to count."

Dallas leaned back and scratched where his hair remained snarled from sleep. "Did Jud usually drop the girls, or did they drop him?"

"A girl'd have to be pretty quick to get out before Jud. I mean she could still be 'reaching for a cigarette'—if you know what I mean—and he'd be out the door."

"What if one of them did, though? What if some woman dropped Jud first? Was he the type to be depressed about it?"

"Jud wasn't the depressed type. Ticked is more likely how he'd be. Insulted."

"I need to find someone who was with Jud within a few days of when he died. To see what kind of mood he was in. What he'd been doing."

"You don't believe me about him not being suicidal." Terry's chin rested on the backs of her hands. She held the end of a fork in her fingertips and let it swing back and forth like a pendulum in a Salvador Dali painting.

"I just want to check around."

"You know the party house?"

"Which one?"

"Bayside around Gold Coast Mall. Sits out on a point. Pool overlooking the bay."

"Sounds pretty nice."

"I saw Jud there a few times. Some of those *flying* nights."

"Jud was high?"

Terry nodded while idly considering another piece of toast.

"On coke?"

Terry said, "I thought, but who knows, maybe he was just high on himself. His attitude was pissing a lot of people off, especially people who'd known him a couple summers."

"I'd like to know the names of those people. The ones Jud was pissing off. Or anyone who might have seen him last week."

"Yeah, okay." Terry waved for their waitress, asked to borrow her pen, and proceeded to jot some names on a General's Kitchen napkin, making her list below the caricature of Gus that had the restaurant's owner cartooned as half man, half chicken. She wrote quickly, as if copying notes from a class she'd missed, sometimes drawing the pen over the soft napkin so abruptly the thin paper wrinkled beneath the ballpoint tip.

"And the address of the party house?" Dallas asked during a pause.

"I'm not sure, but you can't miss that. Any night something's going on it's lit up like a stadium."

"Who's place is it?"

"Somebody who's loaded, because half the time you don't have to bring your own beer. An endless line of kegs keeps on coming." She handed him the list.

Dallas checked her handwriting against his memory. The lettering was abrupt and boxy, no flow to it. Even taking into account the speed of her scribble and that she'd been writing on a napkin, not a flowery notepad, it didn't look like Terry was the one who'd written the *Dear Judson* letter. Not that Dallas suspected her.

1 1

IF SWEATING WERE A national sport, Donny Edson could have
turned pro. Steam pouring through the rear window of the wood shanty
crab shack looked to have lifted the screen clean out of its track. Half
hidden in the spicy-smelling vapor was the soaking-wet Donny Edson.
His sleeveless T-shirt clung to his fleshy chest and made him look like
an angry snake trying to shed a layer of irritating skin.

"How they running?" Dallas asked through the screen.

"Small and light." Edson picked through freshly steamed Maryland
crabs with thick leather gloves already congealed with salt and peppery
spices from previous batches.

Even the crabs looked sweaty, their hard-shell backs glistening red
and moist. Edson tossed them into wooden bins according to size —
medium, large, and jumbo. (Once the price of crabs had risen beyond
$12 a dozen, no one had the nerve to call any of them "smalls"
regardless of actual size.)

"You know Judson Fitch?" Dallas asked the crab steamer.

"Uh-huh." Edson, the first person on Terry's list that Dallas had
been able to locate, didn't sound especially enthusiastic. Although that
may have been because of the hypnotic state of his employment more
than anything else. Steaming crabs would be a great job if you could do
it in a snowstorm — but crabs only run in Maryland during the hottest
months.

"You seen him lately?"

"No. Not going to either. Or so I hear. But who knows?" The kid shrugged meaty shoulders. "It could be a bluff. I don't think I'd believe he was dead 'less I saw the body."

"Why's that?" Dallas stepped back half a pace from the window. Between midafternoon sunshine, summer humidity, and crab steam, it was like being in a hot box.

"Bastard owed me about a hundred bucks." The high temperatures seemed to aggravate the spread of puffy acne that scarred Edson's cheeks.

"For what?"

"Borrowed about fifty off me beginning of summer, then when I asked for it back, he bet me double or nothing on an Orioles' game, and I been after my money ever since."

"You be on the Orioles?"

"Bet on 'em to lose." Edson grunted as he lifted a fresh bushel of live crabs. Pale blue and glistening with seawater, they clawed angrily at the air as Edson popped the wood crate's lid. "You bet the Oh-no's to lose, they're not gonna disappoint you. Farm system's shit and the only guys they trade for are losers. You show me a guy who had an ERA of nine last year, I'll lay even money the O's try an' get him. Some drunken scout'll say, yeah, I remember seeing that guy pitch a good game in A-ball six years ago. I think we can get something out of him."

Dallas always classified baseball along with religion and world politics; he swore never to debate any of those topics with anyone. It was safer to curse someone's family heritage than to argue whether or not Earl Weaver could have won the World Series the year Joe Altobelli did it with the Orioles.

"How come Jud borrowed money from you?"

"I must look like a sucker."

"No, I meant what'd he need the money for?"

Edson dumped the bushel of live crabs into the steamer and covered the huge cast-iron pot, having to fight with the lid to contain a vengeful swirl of steam. "Jud spent lots of money. He liked to live it up. I don't know why he had to get it from me, though, he always said his family was loaded. He bragged about how rich his old man was. Thought that made him a big shot."

Dallas waved off a fat horsefly that settled on his arm. "When was the last time you saw him?"

"Last week. I happened'a be beside him at a light heading downtown. Jud was in his new Jaguar, showing off, tearing around town with some babe beside him. He had the windows up, running the AC, and wouldn't even roll down the window to talk to me. Course I'm sure he knew I was gonna ask about the money and he didn't want the girl to hear. He just smiled — the dick — then burned off the light like dragging me's some kind of accomplishment. Hell, my jeep, it's a good day if it runs. Who'm I gonna race?"

From inside the crab shanty, the manager shouted demandingly, "Edson, where's my two dozen jumbos?"

"Two minutes," Edson shouted, then grabbed a steamed crab from the jumbo bin. Its shell was not quite five and a half inches from point to point. "When I was a kid, my grandfather'd make me throw this back, tell me we'd look for its pop. This guy," his eyes shifted in the direction of his manager's shout, "calls 'em jumbos and sells 'em for twenty-four smacks a dozen. I tell yah, people come in this town, they just oughta throw their money in the bay as they're crossing the bridge. I'm makin' five-fifty an hour, ten hours a day for this jerk. He complains business is slow, and owns a house'd cost me money just to dream about."

Dallas pulled the 280 into the Manager Only parking spot at the Ocean Tides, which, miraculously, was not taken by someone who figured To hell with signs, I'm on vacation.

Before anyone could catch him, he slipped into his apartment through the bathroom window, changed into bathing trunks, then went back out the window and hit the beach.

It was still warm, although a breeze shifting in off the ocean cooled the air along the shoreline. Dallas ran into the water, hurdled some low breakers, and went headfirst through a nice wave.

The ocean was a little choppy with the air flow knocking some size out of the waves, but Dallas still managed a few nice bodysurfing rides before heading back to the hotel. That was all he needed, a little refresher. Just enough to rinse the heat off and bring him back to life. After all, it was close to 4:00 P.M.; the day was about to begin.

"Herbie, what're you doing here?"

"Calculating my overtime."

"You don't get overtime."

"In that case, I'm planning a wildcat strike."

"I'll help you paint some signs." Having showered after his swim, Dallas now wore sweat shorts and a sleeveless yellow T-shirt. His hair was slicked back, clean, but not dried. "Susan leave early?"

"She went out with what's-her-name."

"Teresa Jane?"

"Yeah."

"They weren't looking for me, were they?"

Herbie shook his head.

Dallas started for his office, then stopped and considered his rag-haired night manager. "When you took leave of absence from VPI, did you ever really intend on going back?"

"I might yet." Herbie acted as if there was all the time in the world. He'd graduated high school a year early and took advanced placement courses, so, after only two years at VPI (on a full academic free ride), he was actually further along in credits than some juniors. Maybe he felt far enough ahead to lay back a while. Still, it had been five years . . .

"You really think you could go back at this point? Get into being a student again?"

Herbie considered it deeply, twisting strands of his long, unkempt hair. "With or without a gun to my head?"

"That's what I thought."

On Dallas's desk was a fresh phone message from the county medical examiner, Sam Paul. What a coincidence, Dallas thought, dialing him up.

Dr. Paul's secretary managed to answer the call on the seventh ring. Dallas had never learned her name, he just referred to her as Miss Exasperated.

Sam Paul didn't have that many bodies to deal with, but his secretary still managed to get the most possible agony out of it. She was a lack of efficiency in motion, taking three steps when only one was required, then sighing and moaning to show how overworked she was.

When Dallas asked to talk to Sam, she groaned as though he'd asked her to swim a convoy of Egyptian pyramids across the ocean on her back. Her finger plunked heavily on the hold button.

"The woman needs a raise," were the first words Dallas spoke to the ME. "Whatever you're paying her, it's less than half of what she thinks she's worth."

"Sue's okay," Sam defended her, but he was the charitable type. He'd surrendered a major post in a teaching hospital to assume his present position in Salisbury — all just to raise a family in a small town, away from city temptations.

"I was about to call you when I got your message," Dallas said. "You must have the old voodoo spells working. How'd you know I was interested?"

Sam Paul dabbled with the supernatural now and then, although Dallas was one of the few people to whom he'd ever confessed that he believed corpses occasionally tried to communicate with him. Dallas figured if that was all the loonier Sam Paul got from cutting up dead people, he was ahead of game.

"Actually, Dallas, Chief Dawson said *you* might call *me*. He said I shouldn't tell you anything and to try to find out why you're looking into Judson Fitch's death."

"That sneaky fat bastard."

"I figured you'd want to know. About that *and* the autopsy."

"Thanks." Dallas started looking for a pen, opening desk drawers, finding a letter from the collection agency hired by First Omni Bank to work on his Visa card balance. "Anything odd about how the kid died? Or was it a slam-dunk suicide?"

"Nothing suspicious about his death. You find someone on concrete who's just fallen ten, fifteen floors, it tends to simplify things."

"Any drugs swimming around in his system?"

"Nope. No alcohol, either."

"No THC?" Dallas asked, surprised.

"Nothing. No PCP, heroin, LSD."

"LSD?" Dallas wondered why even mention that narcotic antique; he thought Vietnam era drugs were passé.

"It's making a comeback on cute little comic book papers out of L.A.," Sam threw in as a sidebar.

"What about any signs of drug or alcohol abuse? Not necessarily ingested around the time of death, but recently? Within the last few months?"

"No, but that's tough to call. Like I said, the THC screen was negative, so he probably hadn't done grass in the last couple weeks."

Dallas sighed, renewing his search for the pen on the floor around his desk; there had to be one lying around somewhere. "I don't know, Sam, I heard the kid was a user."

"Could be. But nothing excessive. And his nasals were real clean, so if he did cocaine, it was strictly part-time."

"If it wasn't there, it wasn't there."

"The only thing even close to peculiar about him was a pretty good contusion on the back of his head."

"Well, like you said, he fell, right?"

"He fell facedown," Sam clarified. "Actually, his lower body hit first, absorbing some of the blow, then his shoulders and face. So a knot on the back of the head wouldn't necessarily fit, although he could have hit something, a railing maybe or the wall, on the way down."

"You think he got whacked on the noodle and thrown over the edge?"

"I can't support that, I'm just saying it's the only thing even the least bit out of the ordinary. Nothing more. He could have banged his head getting out of the car or while picking up a napkin he dropped under the dinner table. It could have happened twelve, twenty-four hours before he died. Even longer."

"What about the guy we found under the bed?" Dallas gave up looking for a pen; he'd have to trust his memory, which was about a fifty-fifty shot. "You have a time of death for him?"

"Our John Doe." He was yet to be identified. "Friday night, Saturday morning, in that range. It's hard to be sure unless I could know what the temperature was wherever he'd been until he was found. By the way, good work on that. How'd you come across him?"

"I was delivering some furniture."

"Oh." Sam Paul didn't get it, but since he was a doctor and had all that education under his hat, he didn't like it to seem that he didn't catch on right away.

"The gunshot killed him?"

"Yep."

"Well then," Dallas said with a sigh, "I guess that only leaves one question: Did Jud Fitch's corpse try to send you any memos from the great beyond about being murdered?"

"Nary a one."

$\triangledown$

12

TERESA JANE AND SUSAN got out of Suz's white VW Rabbit. Parked near the far stairs, Susan didn't bother putting up the cabriolet top once she and Teresa Jane lifted shopping bags out of the backseat. The women laughed easily, that spring in their gait Dallas always associated with a post-shopping high; they seemed to be hitting it off well. Dallas only hoped Teresa Jane wasn't going to end up making Susan think she should go back to being a city lawyer.

He could hear them laughing from inside Teresa Jane's room when he was still half a flight of stairs short of the third floor. If the conversation turned yuppie — salaries, job descriptions, mortgage payments — Dallas was going to invite C.J. over to whip up the girls a little Jiffy Pop surprise and smoke them out.

"Knock-knock." Dallas stuck his head in the room.

Teresa Jane was beside the double bed farthest from the door, holding a one-piece bathing suit up against her clothes. Price tags were still hooked to floral-print neoprene.

"I love it," Susan complimented her, sitting on the other bed. With her legs crossed, her skirt slid high up her thigh like an eager caress. "What do you think, Dallas?"

Dallas took that as an invitation to come in. "What's not to like?"

Teresa Jane blushed faintly at the compliment. "I'll try it on, but no remarks about how pale I am." She brushed past Dallas, went into the bathroom, and closed the door, snapping the knob lock.

"So." Dallas sat on the bed beside Susan, put his hand, which she

66

promptly removed, on her exposed knee. "Uh-huh," he sighed. He clapped his own thighs. "Well, I assume you two have been doing girl stuff. No talk about her brother's case, right?"

"Not until you say so." Susan hadn't been crazy about Dallas's idea of keeping Teresa Jane in the dark about the investigation, but Dallas's instincts were generally decent so she was going along with him. "We've just been shopping. Seeing the sights. Talking."

Sunshine through the balcony door cast an even brightness over the room, bringing with it enough heat to keep the air conditioner busy.

"And I'll tell you something, Dallas, I'm glad I wasn't Teresa Jane Fitch growing up." Susan leaned back on her elbows on the bed beside Dallas, a pose that made him want to jump on top of her. The black racer-back tee she wore hugged her breasts fondly. "Her father's a real gem."

"So I've gathered. She say anything about Mom?"

Susan shook her head. "I get the picture her mother stayed pretty much in the background. Probably called her husband 'sir,' that kind of deal."

"Oh, Christ."

Susan scissored her bangs between two fingers and pulled them down toward her eyes, gauging their length, then released them. "And you know why she's really here?"

Dallas looked at her oddly. "About her brother." Like, what was the big secret.

"She's here because she's thought about the same thing." When Dallas didn't catch on, Susan said, "Suicide."

"Come on. Miss Perfect?"

Susan nodded. "She told me once, in college, she took an entire bottle of sleeping pills, figuring that would end it. But her roommate got her to the infirmary in time. She went through therapy for the rest of the semester, then followed up when things got rough again."

"What'd her old man say about that?"

"She kept it from him. The doctors did, too, especially when they realized he was a main cause."

"So how's finding out about her brother going to help?"

"I don't know, exactly, but I think she wants to know what triggered him. If he killed himself, it makes her vulnerable, knowing she might try it again sometime. She doesn't like her life, Dallas, at least that's the feeling I get. It's like her old man forced her into it. So if it turns out that Jud killed himself *because* of their father, she could stick that in his face and make him eat the blame." Susan made it sound as if she didn't think that was such a bad idea.

The bathroom door opened and Teresa Jane emerged in her new swimsuit. She stood awkwardly, arms by her sides, shoulders sloped slightly forward. "Is it okay?" The bottom was cut at an enticing angle over narrow hips, showing off surprisingly nice legs. A V-cut neckline had a bit of a time containing her breasts.

Dallas wondered where she'd gotten that body all of a sudden. He'd figured she was pretty nice, but this! Whatever clothes she'd been wearing, she should sell them to the army; camouflaging that figure seemed about as impossible as hiding a missile in a washbasin.

Teresa Jane was too self-conscious in the new suit to go onto the beach, so instead they sat on the back balcony to catch some late-afternoon sun. Susan even changed into the black-and-red striped bikini she kept in the office.

"Where's that damned butler?" Dallas demanded.

"You have a butler?" Teresa Jane was stretched out on a folding deck chair between Dallas and Susan; her luminescent skin glowing like porcelain.

"Well, sort of." Dallas snuck fond glimpses at the way Susan's nipples toyed with her top. Facing the sun, she had her eyes closed and didn't catch him at his folly. Otherwise, she might've smacked him.

The butler—who was actually Herbie wearing a T-shirt with an imprint of a tuxedo jacket, cummerbund, and bow tie—paced stiff-legged across the parking lot carrying a pitcher of Mai Tais on a cork tray.

"Vite, garçon, vite!" Dallas encouraged him, leaning over the railing.

Herbie was winded by the climb to the third floor, but still managed to neatly fill three rocks glasses with colorful cocktail, dashing in a little extra grenadine for effect. He whipped off something in French—which was actually the name of a Canadian hockey player—then retreated down the stairs with a drink of his own.

They happily drank Mai Tais, à la Herbie, and enjoyed the afternoon. It was a perfect potable prescription that began with summer sun, generous glasses filled with cracked hunks of ice over which was poured pineapple and orange juices, Myers Platinum White Rum, and two splashes of grenadine.

"A good Mai Tai," Dallas offered, "is all in the grenadine."

"Here, here," Susan toasted, hoisting her glass.

Ah, Dallas did love that bikini.

Across the Ocean Tides parking lot and Coastal Highway, Assawoman Bay sparkled bright blue under the late-afternoon sun. The drone of a Jet-Ski engine hummed in the distance; a life-jacketed rider skimmed across shallow wetlands, causing a rippled wake that disturbed terns nesting in the tall sea grass.

Waiting until they had a mild buzz from Herbie's tropical concoction, Dallas braved a toned-down version of the day's events, enough to fill her in without flipping her out. "I talked to some people who knew your brother. Selling drugs has emerged as the front-running way Jud got his newfound wealth."

Teresa Jane remained stoic.

"On the other hand, gambling may have played a hand." When neither woman reacted, Dallas reached around Teresa Jane to playfully jab Susan's bare shoulder. "Hey, get it? Gambling may have *played a hand*."

Susan leaned closer to Teresa Jane. "He's never amazed enough at his own genius sometimes." Susan reached for her Mai Tai.

Teresa Jane tried a smile.

"So," Dallas asked her, "what do you think?"

Teresa Jane considered it. "I don't know."

"Come on," Dallas prodded gently, "you must have some feeling about it. Like an inkblot test. I say Judson's selling cocaine, what's your gut reaction?"

"No," she answered quickly, but then, with great effort, drew aside her blanket of emotional numbness and let an honest answer emerge. "I hope not, but it's possible. It would fit." Slowly, she seemed to realize that denying the truth wouldn't keep it from being so.

"Fit with what?"

"His impatience. That's why he left — took a leave of absence — from school." Teresa Jane shifted positions uncomfortably, as though revealing something negative was as disconcerting as letting her body peak out around the seductive cut of her new one-piece. She spoke slowly, deliberately, measuring words as if they were ingredients in a chemistry experiment. "Judson tended to think he should be able to snap his fingers and get a reaction. Like our father."

Dallas perceived that in some slight way she was condemning both father *and* son.

"Judson never wanted to wait for anything. He didn't understand why he should have to *earn* something if someone — *father* — could have *given* it to him. He couldn't comprehend that money alone isn't a solution."

Dallas raised his hand. "I volunteer to disprove that notion to anyone who wants to quick-fix me with a million bucks."

"What I'm talking about is real-life money, not magic money."

Dallas said, "Magic money?"

"That's what it is to people who don't understand it. They don't really know where money comes from or where it goes." Teresa Jane pulled back her long hair, keeping it from her face. "Where I work, a group in our office deals strictly with professional athletes, managing their money. A baseball player who earns three hundred thousand per annum over a seven-year career is actually less likely to retire comfortably at age sixty-five than a man who earns sixty thousand dollars, adjusted for inflation, over forty years of employment."

Dallas took her word for it. He wasn't into higher math, which he considered to be anything tougher than the addition of a pair of three-digit numbers.

"Unless the ballplayer learns how to use the money, he'll blow it as soon as he makes it, then keep spending at that rate once he's out of the game — selling real estate or getting suckered into backing a restaurant. At which time he'll be making a fourth as much, or even less.

"My father tried to instill in us the sense that having the money is only one step — sometimes the easiest step. There has to be a discipline, a knowledge of how to handle it. What to buy, what not to buy, and not just investments, but cars, homes, clothes, even food. How to keep from letting a champagne appetite dictate to a beer budget."

Dallas turned sideways in his canvas chair to face Teresa Jane straight on. "Did your father give Jud *any* money?"

"We both got ten thousand dollars each Christmas, but Judson's was placed in an educational trust."

"On what terms?"

"He had to maintain a two-point-five to keep his scholarship."

"He had a scholarship?" Dallas was wondering what else her old man could have wanted, then Teresa Jane explained that her father "donated" an amount equal to twenty percent in excess of Jud's tuition each year to the school. Jud got a ride, while the old man got a questionable tax write-off.

"And if his grade average fell?" Dallas wondered.

"If the scholarship was withdrawn — for any reason — Jud's tuition would have come out of the educational trust."

"What if he dropped out?"

"The trust would be wiped out and all the proceeds reverted to my father. Whereas if he stayed and graduated, Jud got to keep the remainder."

So, Dallas calculated, whatever Jud had come into here at the beach, he'd probably have made sure it would cover that spread. Otherwise, there was no sense walking away from money he was within striking distance of collecting upon graduation. Not to mention he'd probably get chucked out of the will.

Teresa Jane stared at her sunset pink drink and swirled it easily. "My father" — she began, then paused for a sip of Mai Tai for courage — "has a dog."

Dallas glanced out to left field to see if that's where this idea had come from.

"It's a pedigree labrador retriever that's the most beautiful golden color. Like . . . wheat," she finally decided.

"Nice dog?" Dallas asked idly, thinking he should play along.

Teresa Jane took another sip of Mai Tai. The deeper she went into the drink, the more sizable her swallows became. "A very nice dog. Very obedient — that's the part my father likes about him the most." She looked at Dallas, sending a message with her eyes. "He's the kind of dog my father can beat when he's bad, and the dog keeps on loving him."

$\triangledown$

13

DALLAS HAD ALMOST FORGOTTEN about Johnny D, the guy the guard at the Atlantis said had been out on the balcony the night Judson fell.

Nicely lit from the Mai Tais, though, Dallas didn't want to chance driving; no sense helping some cop make his DWI quota for the month.

He waited fifteen minutes for the municipal bus, first waving on one of the retired MTA buses the town had taken over from the city of Baltimore. Dallas hated those damned smog-belching buckets of metal.

He preferred the little aluminum death traps with Tonka-toy wheels that looked as if they'd roll over making a fifteen-degree turn. Painted green and white, their seating made a schoolbus seem luxurious. Iron chair backs and squashed vinyl padding were always damp from soaking-wet bathing trunks, even if no one's butt had been on them for two hours (nothing ever dried out in Ocean City; ninety percent humidity wouldn't allow it).

Dallas held on to the seat in front of him as the minibus bounced along the flat road, not even pretending it had shock absorbers. Dallas recognized the driver as someone he'd gotten off on a speeding ticket a few years before. At the time, the kid had more points on his MVA record than some pro basketball teams average per quarter.

At Forty-fourth Street, Dallas started yanking the chain that rang a bell on the driver's console. When the kid didn't stop, Dallas clawed his way to the front of the twenty-seat bus, stepped over a sand-encrusted boogie board, and tapped the driver on the shoulder.

"Jesus Christ!" The driver jumped in his seat. "You trying to scare me to death. I'm driving here."

The bus sort of glided off path, from the bus lane into the slow lane. Ashley—"Crashly"—that was the driver's name, Dallas remembered now. He had long red-brown hair and didn't seem to hear the angry chorus of horns that followed the bus wherever he drove it. Maybe he thought it was always New Year's.

Ashley switched abruptly back into the bus lane, cutting off a green TR7 in the process. The way Ashley drove, phone poles set five feet off the road were obstacles to be feared.

"Stop the world, Ash, I want to get off."

Ashley blinked at him, then searched for the brake with panicky jabs of his foot. "Hey, you're the lawyer." He had the bus crawling along slowly now.

Dallas considered making a jump for it. "That's right."

"Great, I been meaning to call you but I forgot your name." Ashley dug into a pouch beside his seat and came out with a fistful of traffic citations. "I got all these State of Maryland gift certificates here. Think we can do something with them?"

"How 'bout kindling?" Dallas grabbed the door handle and pulled it sharply. The double door unfolded with a quiet swish. With the bus trolling at 8 mph, Dallas lunged for the sidewalk.

Dallas recognized the red baggies the guard had described. There was also a red bandanna around Johnny D's throat and each of his wrists.

Out in the surf, the thick kid paddled smoothly, aiming the nose of a turquoise surfboard along the clean face of a building wave. Sensing that he was in the flow of it, he moved quickly up onto the board, feet planted perfectly. He made one adept adjustment of balance, then fishtailed the board to get more action out of a minor-league tube. As soon as the breaker turned over, Johnny D snapped his board off the crest of the wave and jumped into the water.

It was getting toward 7:30, Dallas's time of day. The beach was winding down. Most of the tourists had surrendered the beach, returning to their rooms to shower, then fight traffic down to boomtown or to stand in line at Phillips' for steamed crabs and flounder.

Dallas was outside the Ocean Club, beneath a cluster of migrated palm trees that were doomed to perish as soon as the first fall chill hit the air. It seemed like a ridiculous practice, digging up trees from some Florida nursery and moving them as far north as Maryland. They looked good for a couple weeks, then faded. Although once the palm trees died, some of Ocean City's more inventive — and frugal — entrepreneurs gathered up fallen branches, spray-painted them green, and stapled them back on the dead trunks. It was a harmless little fraud.

A sharp rap against the smoked glass Ocean Club window got Dallas's attention. Smiling from inside the bar was Carl Peters, the proverbial amiable beach bartender, inviting Dallas in with a freshly uncapped bottle of beer.

"Here on business," Dallas called loudly enough to be heard through the tall window.

Carl gave him a yeah-right nod and turned back to his Happy Hour patrons.

Dallas leaned against the glass wall and enjoyed the shade, watching Johnny D work what he could out of small waves.

Forty-fifth Street was purposefully jettied to improve what were more often than not disappointing East Coast breakers. It was especially rough at high tide, when what waves there were pounded directly onto packed sand, making for a rough ride and sure nose smasher.

It didn't take long for Johnny D to call it a day. He came ashore with his turquoise board under his arm, running his fingers over a wide skull of bristlelike hair. He jogged easily toward the stone jetty, picked up a towel without breaking stride, and continued toward Forty-fourth Street.

Dallas caught up with him as he was securing his board to the roof rack of a reclaimed post office jeep painted in desert camouflage — a sort of nouveau–Afrika Korps motif.

"Not much in the way of waves, huh?"

Johnny D peered at Dallas with stony blue eyes set beneath a protruding forehead. He looked like a Malibu Neanderthal. The bridge of his nose was peeling and reddish pink from too much sun. He looked to have spent most of his twenty-two years doing isometrics; he wasn't overmuscled, but lean and powerful, the kind of kid who could chase someone for five miles on foot and still have plenty of endurance to beat the hell out of him.

Saying nothing, Johnny D continued securing a nylon webbed strap tightly around his board as if it was serious business.

Dallas wondered what the deal was with all the red bandannas — one around the throat he could see as playing it semicool, but doing each wrist, too? "Guy said you were at a party up the Atlantis the other night. When that kid jumped."

74

Johnny D yanked a second strap into place, then rapped the board with the butt of his fist to make sure it wasn't going anywhere.

"That you were out on the balcony, so I thought maybe you saw something."

Johnny D turned toward Dallas, crossing his arms to make his biceps bulge. His stomach was defined with hard ridges like an oyster shell. "Wuddn't me." He had the deep, lazy voice of someone who wanted people to think he was from California.

"You weren't there?"

"Nope."

"You sure?"

"Look, man, you a cop? I mean, you don' look like no cop."

"I'm not a cop, I just wanted to know—"

"Then get the hell outta my face."

Dallas stepped back, hands out to his sides—the gesture saying, okay, no problem—figuring if he didn't, Johnny D was going to help him in a none-too-charitable way.

$\bigtriangledown$

14

"**W**HO TAUGHT YOU to iron?" Half a gooey cheese steak sub hung from Herbie's hand as he watched Dallas do battle with a travel iron.

The compact appliance hissed meanly as Dallas dragged it across a button-down shirt he'd found buried in the closet. His version of an ironing board was the kitchen table spread with two thick issues of *Beachcomber*, the resort town's weekly advertiser.

"There's gotta be an easier way," Dallas complained.

"Wear T-shirts." A glob of mayonnaise chased two strands of fried onion from his sub and landed on the floor; Herbie nudged it under a heat vent with a bare toe.

"We're going someplace nice. It's her treat." Dallas tried to make it sound as if he wasn't really interested.

"Oh, you and Lady Ice . . . that is nice." Herbie grinned sarcastically.

Dallas had been working on the shirt so long, he'd just about ironed the stripes out of it. His eyes were beginning to play tricks on him; he could no longer tell the front of the garment from the back, or had he welded them together?

"You ready for a theoretical question?" Dallas proposed, tilting the iron on its side, taking a break.

Herbie was in charge of theories around the Ocean Tides. "Shoot."

"Let's pretend you're in college. A junior. And if you don't graduate, you might be disinherited from a very rich family." Dallas admired how well he'd ironed the shirt cuff. He was good at cuffs. "Then again, even once you do graduate, you might have to wait — who knows? — ten, twenty, thirty years to collect your inheritance."

"How come I've gotta wait?"

"Well, your parents aren't dead yet."

"My aunt's real sick, does that count?"

"No." Dallas took a breath. "What I want to know is, would you have finished school, then been a 'good boy' for as long as it took for the will to make you rich?"

"Probably not." Herbie didn't need long at all to think about that.

"How come?"

"Boss, this is the age of pessimistic youth. We don't really expect the world to last that long. Put off fun today, you might die to regret it tomorrow when someone hits the wrong button and starts World War Last."

Teresa Jane Fitch wasn't eating her lobster. It was sitting perfectly, enticingly on a bed of soft Bibb lettuce, all glossy red and steamy, with succulent tail meat already prompted from its moist shell. A glass tub of clarified butter was waiting patiently to receive hunks of cracked claw to make it even tastier.

Dallas was salivating just looking at it. If he'd known she was getting lobster, he'd have ordered it, too. But since she was paying, he'd kept the price down and ordered soft-shell crabs, which had been delicately coated with flour, spices, and pan-fried a golden brown, but, hell, it wasn't lobster. And that she *had* ordered lobster now made his soft-shell crabs seem like a soggy layer of yesterday's Wheaties. That she wasn't *eating* the lobster was making him crazy.

What she was doing was drinking. More Mai Tais. Two at the bar while they'd waited for a table. One more after they'd been seated at their ocean-view table. Inebriation-wise, Teresa Jane was on the Good Ship Lollypop.

"Why haven't you ever been married?" she asked again. The tulip glass tilted in her fingers.

If she spilled any fruity Mai Tai onto the lobster, Dallas was going to swear out a warrant for her arrest. It would have been gastronomically criminal.

"You certainly seem marry-able." She managed to keep her words steady, not a slur in sight, though her eyes were getting that dreamy-drinky quality to them, seeming a little far away.

"You've gotta be kidding?" She was, wasn't she? How had the

conversation turned from Judson's sudden life-style change to Dallas never marrying. There must've been a cut-off Dallas missed on the map.

"Do you know . . . no one's ever asked me to marry him?" Her shoulders tilted slightly, the most relaxed pose Dallas had ever seen her manage. Teresa Jane didn't even seem to care anymore how pale her skin looked in the strapless dress (she hadn't wanted to wear it, but Susan had insisted). "Not one person. Not even" — she looked around for the right word, as if it were a bug flying around her face — "a geek. Someone I wouldn't want to marry."

"You're young yet." Dallas tried to be soothing, but he wondered how old she was going to be before she started in on that lobster.

"The man at the carnival thought I was thirty-five."

"Thirty-five isn't old. Trust me."

She looked at him almost slyly, watching around the rim of her glass as she sipped more Mai Tai. "I do," she said with lips moist from her drink, "trust you." Her dreamy eyes considered him, then, suddenly, closed. Teresa Jane set her drink down quickly. She grasped the linen tablecloth to steady herself. "Mmm." She swayed slightly. "Oh, God. I've had way too much to drink." She laughed quietly, touched the floral print fabric that cupped her breasts. "This is embarrassing. I'm sorry."

Dallas smiled. "What the hell. Are you having a good time?"

She laughed again, a little too loudly this time, then whispered to make up for it. "I'm having a great time." As she leaned forward, Dallas couldn't help liking the way she looked in that dress. And he couldn't believe what he was thinking, considering . . .

He looked away and tried to recapture his first impression of Teresa Jane Fitch, all starched and professional in his office, coming off like a ramrod in a bow tie. It was hard to imagine how this sea change had come over her.

Then again, sometimes the beach was a dangerous place. There was a sense of detachment from the real world that made people do things they wouldn't even consider back home. That's what Dallas liked about it.

Still, it surprised him when Teresa Jane's hand reached across the table and came to rest warmly on his. "Why don't you care?" she asked, trying to be sober.

"What d'you mean?"

She separated his fingers, played with them. "Do you care . . . about anything?"

"Lots of things."

"What? Not money."

"Money can be very disappointing sometimes. Not often," Dallas tempered, "but sometimes."

"I know what you mean," she replied, sloshily agreeable.

"It can disillusion you faster than people."

"Is that why you're not married? Because you're disillusioned?" She had a little bit of a tussle with that word.

"Marriage," Dallas said, "is the beginning of old age. It's the crest of that slippery slope of reality no amount of sports cars, toupees, or pukka shells can rescue."

"Do you . . . go with anyone?"

Dallas shook his head.

"So, there's no one . . . Do you have family?"

"Sure." His answer was sincere. The lobster was getting cold, but he liked the way she touched his hand. There was a gentleness he hadn't expected from her.

"But what do you care about?" The conversation seemed to have hopped a semidrunken merry-go-round, where thoughts strolled in and out of Teresa Jane's head like glossily painted horses bobbing on a metal pole. "Do you care about me?"

"Yeah."

She glanced down. A strand of chestnut hair came loose from its braid and lay across her left eye. "That wasn't convincing." She looked up. "So try again. I'm in a convincible mood."

Driving back to the motel, Teresa Jane was asleep within ten blocks of the restaurant.

At the Ocean Tides, Dallas carried her up the stairs to her room. He put her and her new strapless dress under the covers and turned off the light.

He adjusted the air conditioner to make sure it would remain cool overnight, locked the door, and went back to his car. There, he retrieved the carryout bag with the cartoon of a hungry-looking hound dog on the side.

Now he'd eat lobster.

The party house was the kind of place MBA students dreamed about in their richest, most perverse spells of slumber. Situated on a narrow point overlooking the bay, the slickly designed home cast bright reflections across dark water as halogen lights lit the place up like fireworks.

Four separate, steeply angled cedar-shake roofs alternated heights over distinct sections of the house. Arched, clerestory windows glowed bright yellow with interior light.

Nearly every square foot of the property — inside and out — was alive with the party. Indoors, people moved freely from room to room; outside they cavorted across the minimalist landscaped yard, drinking beer beneath party tents.

This was the place Terry had told Dallas about.

Dallas squeezed into a parking spot on the lawn and found himself overwhelmed by the crowd as he got out of the car. It was hard to guess with everyone moving about, making lots of noise, but he guessed there were at least four hundred in attendance. Mostly, it was a young college crowd.

Near the bulkhead that guarded the point from high tides, three guys cheered on a short-haired blonde in a wet bathing suit. One guy held an inch-wide plastic tube in her mouth, while another raised up the funnel end and poured in a freshly popped can of beer. A deep chorus of "Go-go-go!" encouraged her to quickly gulp the rush of suds. That accomplished, she raised her arms victoriously. The guys picked her up over their heads and carried her off, bellowing, "Ugha-ugha-ugha!" as though celebrating the queen of the Nile.

Dallas wished he had a buck for every time someone chanted go-go-go — or ugha-ugha-ugha — any given night in Ocean City. He'd be so wealthy he could probably buy out Teresa Jane's father.

Dallas walked across the straight leg of a U-shaped driveway to one of the party tents. Lots of young eyes looked to see if he was someone familiar, usually turning slightly cold and distant when he wasn't. Occasionally he'd get a smile just seeming happy-go-lucky, as if he'd stumbled into nirvana from a post–age thirty haze.

The beer was on tap and free, served in oversized plastic cups.

"Amazing these people can afford it?" Dallas raised his cup to a kid leaning against a tent pole. "Free beer."

"Yeah, and no ID, either." The kid was blond and freckled and seemed glad to have someone to talk to. He eyed a cute girl, but never moved from the pole. His breath smelled like the beer, which suddenly made Dallas lose a little of his taste for it. "Guy owns this place is loaded."

"I don't know him. He around?" Dallas looked for someone who might be rich.

There were quite a few candidates, but all were too young. Whatever happened to the days when college kids wore raggy-assed jeans, ripped

T-shirts, and suede vests with fringe? Most of this crowd had on fifty-dollar shirts. There were even a few Rolexes strapped on athletic wrists.

"Dude doesn't come to his own parties. But they say he watches. From up there." The kid nodded toward the highest of the four roof peaks, where a six-sided crow's nest was perched above the lights, almost hidden in darkness.

Shading his eyes from the halogens' glare, Dallas saw tall, dark windows on all three walls visible to him. The roof peak sported a polished weathervane that reflected a hint of golden light.

The kid said, "Guy I know met him once. Says he's sort of odd-looking, like he had some kind of illness. But he's okay now. He's supposed to pick out the best-looking girl who shows, then invite her up there. This one girl, really hot, I forget her name, but I heard her talking once that the guy just asked her to take off her clothes for him — you know, strip — and he gave her a thousand bucks. Just to look at her."

"Yeah?" Dallas kept looking at the crow's nest.

"First thousand bucks I get?" the kid nodded confidently. "That's what I'm gonna do. Buy me a girl — a woman."

"Great." Dallas walked on. Male-female relations were making such progress.

He made his way around back, where a piered triangle jutted into the bay. A free-form swimming pool was being splashed wildly as body-to-body beer drinkers played dunking games. A few intense chicken fights were going on, girls on guys' backs trying to knock off other girls; lots of playful twisting of bikini tops and underwater grab-assing helped the cause.

"Some party," Dallas said to two girls who seemed to be considering a jump in the pool.

"Yeah, it's great!" The girl was cute, but still had braces.

Getting a better look at her, Dallas guessed she was thirteen. There was no way in hell he'd ever make a move on someone her age, so why was his mind compelled to consider that he'd been over twenty when she was born? His spirit groaned.

"This your house?" the one without braces asked as she danced easily to the music. She looked about the same age and drank beer like a sailor back from three months at sea.

"I thought it was yours." Dallas moved on.

"Know where I can score some of that?" he asked a guy who passed him smoking a joint.

"I got it from someone said he bought it off the guy owns the house."
The toker's fingertips were scorched from smoking every last spliff
down to edible roach. "Primo stuff, too, man. Guy's got a place down
Jamaica he grows the stuff."

"The owner?"

"Yeah. Guy's a heavy-duty Latino. Very connected." He leaned
close to Dallas and waved his hand from side to side, like this was really
shady conversation, keep it to yourself. "Can get you *anything*. But he's
very private. Like that Howard Hughes. And's hardly ever here. Just
uses this place to crash between drug runs. Like a hideout 'cause the
Feds won't come all the way out here."

"Ah." Dallas acted as if the guy had something there. This, he
considered once again, was why most small-time dopers got caught. It
was misconceptions such as the DEA couldn't find Ocean City that got
idiots busted.

The doper walked on. His jeans were slung down his skinny hips so
far the pants legs bagged around his bare feet.

Dallas drank his beer and went inside the house, entering through
a sun room where ten kids in their late teens were crowded in a
steaming hot tub. They passed around liter bottles of wine coolers.

"No room, dude!" one of them called as Dallas continued on.

In the living room, MTV was showing on a wide-screen TV. The
sound boomed through four Bose speakers positioned strategically to
gain the best bass response. A red-and-green Art Deco vase danced
on a brass baker's rack from vibration while a dozen partiers did
likewise across thick pile carpeting.

In the hall, two high school girls in near-matching mini skirts and
teased haircuts pounded impatiently on the bathroom door. Inside,
somebody was heaving his guts into the toilet.

"Either of you know Jud Fitch?" Dallas asked. "I've been looking
for him all—"

"Too bad," the one with the shorter skirt smirked. "He killed himself
last week."

"You're kidding?"

"Come on, Jens, let's try the one upstairs." The other girl pulled on
her friend's top.

"I mean, I don't mean to seem cold, but he had turned into a real
shit. Know what I mean?" Jens—or whatever her name was—blew
upward through pursed lips to lift her bangs away from her eyes. "To
think I even dated the guy once."

"*Jens* . . . ?" The other girl opened her eyes wide with exasperation, then glanced toward the steps to the second floor. "Like I really, *really*, gotta go," she said urgently.

"Okay, so go." Jens shooed her upstairs, then shook her head. "Christ, you get a place down here for the summer, every jerky friend from school thinks it's a drop whenever they want to buzz into town. Eat all your food — don't contribute a dime — then expect you to show them all the hot spots." She looked at her watch. "I gotta get up at six to go to work."

Dallas knew how that went. "You want something to drink?"

She wondered if this was a pass.

"I need to find out something about Jud."

"Yeah. Okay. They've got coolers at the bar. In the kitchen," she directed when Dallas wasn't sure which way to go.

"I guess, really, I miss him. I think I'm mad that he's dead." Jens's full name was Jennifer Lynn Tolly; her most recent claim to fame was having been student council president of Centennial High's latest graduating class.

She sat with Dallas on a bulkhead near the fence that separated the party house from a darkened A-frame next door. Her T-shirt had wide armholes and as she leaned her elbows on drawn-up knees, she — either willingly or not — offered Dallas a free show of small breasts he wasn't too proud not to accept.

"Jud used to be really nice. Someone you could trust. I mean, he'd see other girls, we were nothing steady, but word never got around to other people about what we did together. I mean, some guys, you're with them one night, all their friends start hitting on you because they think you're easy."

"So what happened?"

"I don't know." She rested her head thoughtfully on her knee, looking more like her daddy's twelve-year-old than someone worried about other people finding out what she and her boyfriend did to-gether.

"Jud seemed to, I don't know, sort of come apart. One night, I was with another guy — someone from school — and Jud saw us in the parking lot of this club. Brian was driving a Mercedes — his dad's car, you know. Lots of kids do that, it's no big deal, it wasn't like he was flaunting it or anything. But Jud sees us and comes running over and gets into it with Brian. Wants to know who he thinks he's impressing driving his old man's car. Jud starts poking him, wants to know how much Brian's father makes. What kind of job he has. Where he lives. I mean, it was really weird."

Jens sat up; so much for Dallas's view. "Brian tried to walk away—both of us did—but Jud kept up. He was right in our faces. I mean, it was obvious he wanted a fight, but for what? When he couldn't get Brian to take the first swing, Jud started on me. Asking what I was doing with some guy who's trying to pretend he's rich. That if I wanted to fuck someone with money, I could always fuck him."

She laughed sarcastically. "*That* put Brian off. He nailed Jud—right here." She laid a soft fist to her temple. "*Baboom*. Jud went down like he'd fallen off a skateboard. I mean, the punch was obvious, Jud saw it coming, but he didn't react. Like he wanted to be hit." Jens stared across the bay where the lights of the party house shimmered against the smooth water. "Maybe it was because his father was in town."

"Whose father?"

"Jud's. Mr. Fitch."

"Jud's father was here? When?" Teresa Jane had said Jud was the only one in her family who still came to Ocean City.

"Four or five weeks ago, I guess. The beginning of the season."

"You saw him?"

"Jud introduced us. At first I thought it was going to be this guy Polo Jud had been hanging out with."

"Polo?"

"That's who owns this house."

Dallas would get back to that. "Tell me about his father."

"I don't know. What's to tell? He was his father. Looks like anybody's dad would if he had a lot of money." Jens laughed. "Although it was kind of funny, he had on a suit at the beach. A black suit."

"What was he doing here?"

"I don't know," Jens replied, like how should she know. "I only saw him for about thirty seconds. He and Jud were having one of those discussions, one of those parent-kid *things*." She rolled her eyes as though having suffered her fair share of them as well. "He was probably griping Jud's ass about something from the way Jud talked about him. I mean the guy didn't look like a free thinker, you know. He looked worried."

"Worried about what?"

"I don't know. Just worried. Like all parents look."

Dallas found a stone in the grass and pitched it into the bay where it landed with a silent plunk. He wondered if he'd look worried if he had a daughter like Jens or a son like Jud or a daughter or son like anybody; but the thought of being a parent was so unthinkable he never came upon an answer. Talk about responsibility—Dallas could barely handle running a one-star motel.

Dallas asked Jens if she thought Jud had been selling drugs.

"Everybody said so, but I never saw it. I mean, sure, he'd pass some onto friends, sometimes for money, sometimes not, but everybody does that. I guess he could have been moving some, though. He sure seemed to get awful thick with bucks awful fast. But he'd been hanging around with Polo, so who knows what the money was for? The guy might've just liked Jud, but I didn't think Jud was the type. Even for money."

"Type for what?"

"Hey, don't you know? Polo's queer."

"You know him?"

"No, but one of the girl's in my apartment? Her boyfriend met him. Polo owns a lot of land up in Rehobeth and comes down here stalking new boyfriends." She made a distasteful face. "God, yuk, can you imagine that?"

Dallas was on his way back to his car when a voice called him from the darkness.

"Didn't get what you were after?" the anonymous person asked.

Dallas spotted a camouflage jeep with a red bandanna tied to the antenna. Johnny D.

"You looking to score some grass?" He sounded slightly more friendly than on the beach, but not much.

Dallas shifted into the role of drug buyer. He glanced suspiciously from side to side, making his way through a line of cars to where Johnny D stood against his jeep. "You got—?" Dallas peered at him closely, as if he was surprised who it was. "Wait, I know you."

"The beach today. You were asking about some guy."

"Right. Jud Fitch."

Johnny D rubbed the heel of one docksider against the toe of the other as if he were giving himself a shoe shine. "How come you want to know about him?"

Dallas decided to wing it. "I'll tell yah, I gave the kid a five-hundred-buck deposit for an order and the next thing I know someone say's he's dead. Which I don't buy. I think maybe he was taking lots of orders and then decided to split with the money."

"Don't you read the papers? They said he's dead."

"Maybe Juddie boy just makes it look that way."

Johnny D laughed as if Dallas was stupid. "You think he jumps off a building, lands facedown, and *pretends* to be dead?"

"Maybe it's someone else. Maybe Jud's still alive. I called the cops. They said no one had officially ID'ed the body yet. Only a driver's license in his wallet. No money." Making it all up, Dallas grinned like, see there?

Johnny D made a sour smile, shook his head from side to side. "Your boy's dead. You want to make a new deal, come around here tomorrow."

"What time you gonna be here?"

"I'm not." Johnny D neatened the bandannas tied to each wrist like a tourniquet. "But you come by—anytime—someone'll take care of you."

"You ready for this?" Dallas asked Herbie.

Herbie was in the Ocean Tides office, his feet on Dallas's desk, reading last week's *National Enquirer*.

"New motives." Dallas started counting them off on his fingers. "Jud Fitch was hanging out with a guy who owns a million-dollar house in the capacity of the guy's, *a*, drug runner, *b*, homosexual lover, or, *c*, pimp."

Herbie turned the *Enquirer* inside out and pointed to the headline he read aloud. " 'Aliens Kidnap Teenagers. Turn them into slaves for Martian space station.' "

Dallas nodded thoughtfully. "Equally possible."

$\triangledown$

1 5

NOTHING GOOD EVER HAPPENS before twelve noon. It was not a steadfast rule, but one that Dallas Henry tried to live by—a feat accomplished by sleeping as far into the early afternoon as the real world would allow.

As luck would have it, Dallas awakened naturally on Thursday. It was ten past one.

"You really hit the ground running this morning," Susan said as Dallas stumbled into the Ocean Tides lobby.

"Be nice." The sound of a voice made his head moan.

"You hungover, too? I already took some aspirin up to T.J."

"I am not hungover. It's just early." He started to look for something behind the counter, then stopped. "Who's T.J.?"

"Teresa Jane. It was her school nickname. She said life hasn't been the same since her friends stopped calling her that."

Dallas couldn't imagine why. Maybe that's why no one had ever proposed to her. By the time they got her name out, they forgot what they were going to ask.

Susan watched Dallas root through the file drawers. "I almost hate to ask what you two got into last night."

"I didn't get *into* anything."

"You sound disappointed."

"No. Damn." He stood upright after a fruitless search through the bottom drawer. "Is this going to be the kind of day where I can't find a goddamned thing?"

"Ow," Susan mocked. "My we wake up grouchy when we didn't get any the night before."

"Wait a minute . . . I was . . . it's not what—not like that. I wasn't *trying* to get anything. It was dinner. We went to dinner."

"Fine." Susan smiled like no way she believed that.

"It was *just* dinner." Dallas made a safe signal with his arms like a base umpire. "Okay? Dinner."

"Okay." She kept smiling. "So what are you looking for?"

"Something to use to forge a will."

"It's rather unusual for someone so young to prepare a will, isn't it?" The lady bank manager at Coastal Savings and Loan examined the document that was still warm from the Ocean Tides IBM Selectric. She wore schoolteacher horn-rims that made her look fifty-five instead of forty. "Has this been filed with the Register of Wills, yet?"

"No." Dallas reminded himself to remain seated upright in the vinyl chair as he faced the austere manager. "We're not sure of the amount of assets, so there may not be a need to open an estate." He put on that professionally impatient voice they teach in first-year law; it's designed to stop people who only know a little about the legal system from asking questions, because eventually they'll come up with one you can't answer.

It seemed to appease her. "Actually, this makes it simpler for us." She handed back the four typed pages that had been neatly stapled inside a pale blue folder. "If we can turn matters over to an executor." On the wall to the woman's right was a group photograph of some pretty ugly people Dallas assumed were her family; an alert-eared German shepherd was by far the best-looking of the lot. "So, what was it again that you needed?"

"Just a list of Judson Fitch's accounts here. And the balances."

"Oh, that's all?" Like, she could do that. The woman, Mrs. Bendaman, swiveled her executive chair toward a computer terminal.

Thick wires ran from the machine to a crude hole cut in the wall at about eye level. Dallas imagined the lines as shooting off somewhere magical. That was how he figured computers worked.

With deft fingers, Mrs. Bendaman jabbed a quick entry across the keyboard, then waited stiff-backed for a response. "Good thing you didn't come by yesterday. We were down for five hours."

The computer screen flipped images and a blinking cursor lit beneath two lines of data on a pale green screen. "Here we are. Account five-seven-oh-oh-nine-six-oh-three. Forty-three thousand, one-hundred, twenty-nine dollars and thirty-five cents." She smiled with pursed lips. "Looks like you'll have to open that estate, Mr. Henry."

Dallas tried not to go into shock as he jotted the figure on a legal pad. For an evidentiary fishing expedition, he was doing okay. Like landing a marlin without bait. There had been some blank deposit slips from this bank in the personal papers of Jud's he'd snagged from the kid's condo, but no hint he'd find this kind of cache. Surprised by his find, Dallas tried to think fast.

"I don't believe this." He feigned a professional groan—he'd learned that in second-year law.

"What's the matter?"

"This dumb kid. If it's what I think, this money was supposed to have been placed into a joint account. His father is going to hit the roof. We're going to have IRS problems like you wouldn't believe."

The woman was sympathetic. Mentioning the IRS was a universal way to get someone's compassion; it was more tear-jerking than watching *Bambi*.

Dallas said, nice and polite, "Could I bother you for copies of the account's most recent statements? If I could see when the deposits were made it could be a huge help. Otherwise we've got tax liability you wouldn't believe."

She considered the screen. "The account is only two months old, it shouldn't take long." She left her glass-walled office to voyage into the main body of the small bank. Her rear end was so round, Dallas wondered how she could sit down without rolling over.

In less than fifteen minutes, Mrs. Bendaman came back with a computer statement and what looked to be a credit card. The printout showed that beginning June 22, $3,400 per day—cash—had been deposited for twelve straights days into a variable rate NOW account.

Apparently, Jud Fitch knew about bank reporting regs; any transaction over $3,500 was automatically reported to the Feds. If the money had started out as a lump sum, spacing its deposit over twelve days kept the IRS et al. from finding out.

After that there were no deposits. Only withdrawals, almost one per day, each coded ATM. Usually $400 was taken out, up until and including the day Jud Fitch died: that Friday, $400 had been withdrawn, again coded ATM, at 3:17 P.M.

Dallas said, "I assume ATM means it was an automated transaction."

"Automated teller machine. Bank-in-the-wall. Twenty-four-hour teller. Whatever you want to call it." She handed Dallas what he'd thought was a credit card. "That's what this is." An ATM card was embossed with Jud's name. "The bank places a four-hundred-dollar daily limit on withdrawals. And this particular card was last used to access the account on"—she peered through bifocal horn-rims to check the statement Dallas had in his hand—"let's see, that would be last Friday night just before midnight. But the card was seized by the machine when the PIN code was incorrectly entered after three tries."

"So the card was stolen?"

"Not usually. Most times the account holder is in a hurry or forgets their password. They punch the wrong buttons without realizing the machine keeps the card after three misses. Usually they come in the next day to pick up their card. But Mr. Fitch didn't."

Yeah, Dallas thought, a little fall took care of that.

The electronic age was a wonderful thing. Dallas had to drive half an hour to Salisbury, but it was worth the trip. The private firm handling the security contract for Coastal Savings and Loan maintained a regional office there. Dallas had recovered a substantial sum of money for one of the firm's clients a few years back, which pretty much ensured they'd do whatever they could to return a favor.

In a cool, well-air-conditioned room equipped with a dozen Sony TV screens mounted behind a metal wall plate, Dallas was shown the ATM surveillance tape for Coastal's Ocean City branch office. The tape had been filmed on closed-circuit equipment the night Jud's card was seized by the twenty-four-hour teller.

Jud Fitch was not on the film, but Dallas hadn't expected him to be. If Jud had already withdrawn the daily limit earlier on Friday, going back to the machine would be useless; it wouldn't surrender any more money and Jud would know that. Someone else wouldn't.

The image that appeared on the tape was that of a young woman with shoulder-length dark hair. The exact color couldn't be ascertained because the film quality was grainy black and white. The tape had a jerky quality about it—like a silent movie—because the closed-circuit equipment only fired a shot every half second. Still, the girl's apprehension was evident.

After rushing into the enclosure that housed the wall teller, she had to reinsert the card twice before the machine would even accept it. Then, pulling up the sleeve of a baggy windbreaker, she began frantically hitting buttons to enter the password, clutching tight fists when her attempts failed, finally banging the machine, yelling at it, it seemed, when the bank-in-the-wall ate the card and refused to give it up. When the girl finally left the bank, she did so running.

"There's also this." The young Bahamian man operating the equipment reached across the control panel after he ran the tape a second time. He punched another button and a second screen showed a close-up of the girl's hands shot from above the ATM digit pad. "It probably won't be much help, because there wasn't any money transacted." He spoke carefully, trying to suppress his island accent. "But you'd be surprised how many people claim the machine short-changed them, so we run this film for them, show the money actually coming out of the cash box into their hands."

The guy in the security uniform was right. No money was dispersed, but when the girl pushed up the windbreaker sleeve, there were three old-fashioned bangle bracelets on her wrist. Something that might help down the line, because from just looking at the grainy image of her face, she could have been any one of a hundred girls Dallas might pass strolling the beach.

$\triangledown$

16

DALLAS HOPED HE HADN'T blown it.

Last night, Johnny D said someone would be at the party house today. With any luck, that included late afternoon. One problem with sleeping in was that half the day was over by the time Dallas set foot out of bed. (Actually, was that a problem? Or a benefit?)

Dallas drove around the sweeping curve toward the bay. Elbow out the window, a hot breeze fanned open his Hawaiian-print shirt, the one that made him feel a little like Jack Lord. Book 'em, Danno.

A Toyota 4-Runner sat at an angle in the party house driveway. It had Maryland plates and was covered with a layer of salt residue as though usually parked near the ocean. A half-torn bumper sticker had the imprint LOCAL in block letters beneath a graphic wave.

Dallas left the 280 parked behind the Toyota and got out. A glance inside the Toyota's cab revealed sandy floorboards and an opened pack of Sticklets gum. There were over 30,000 miles on the speedometer. The tires were new. Paint was holding up well. Dallas wondered what the guy would want to sell it.

Remembering to glance over his shoulder — this was, after all, supposed to be a drug run, no casual affair — Dallas went up two brick steps and rang the bell. Waiting, he ran his finger along ornate wood scrolling that had been shellacked and buffed to a rich luster.

When no one answered, he rang the bell again.

"Hey!" A good-looking kid, about twenty years old, jogged around the side of the house. Suntanned to a dark sienna, he was bare chested, wearing blue surfer trunks. "I thought I heard somebody." Barely winded, he glanced toward the door. "Nobody's home."

"You're here."

"Pool boy." He smiled perfect teeth as if he was proud of his job.

"Did they leave a message . . . in case someone stopped by?"

The kid shrugged. "No, but they don't usually have company. Except the parties. Were you supposed to meet Mr. or Mrs. Wiseman? Or the daughter, right?" His smile widened. "You're here to see the daughter."

"Uh . . . "

"She *is* hot. If her parents knew what went on in this place while they were away it'd be holy hell." The kid started to laugh. "But I don't have to tell you."

"No, not me. You don't have to tell me." Dallas thought, so much for the wild stories about drug-running Latinos and sex-crazed old men. He should have known better than to listen to a bunch of kids. But if this place was owned by a family, what the hell had Johnny D set him up with? Some kind of joke?

"Listen." The kid wiped a hand over his strong, hairless chest. "I gotta get the pool finished, but if you want to come around and take a swim . . . ? Maybe Lisa'll be back soon."

"Sure." Dallas figured to get a better look at the place in the daytime. As it was, he hardly recognized it.

The huge tents that had been pitched last night were gone, as was the endless carpet of discarded beer cups thrown over the lawn. Lisa must have sprung for a professional cleaning crew. No way she and a few friends could have tidied up this well.

"My name's Adam." The pool boy hotfooted it over black macadam. Hitting a row of pebbles didn't seem to throw his gait, the sign of feet well blistered by the routines of summers.

"I'm Dallas."

Adam wasn't particularly muscular, but whatever time he spent lifting weights, if any, was concentrated on his upper body and arms. His stomach was lean enough to show a lack of overindulgence, but didn't have that rippled look of someone who could do a hundred sit-ups on command.

Around back by the pool, Adam tended to the vacuum, slowly pushing a long, aluminum pole through silky water like a Venetian waterman steering his gondola. On a pool chair was a wet towel and red T-shirt; there was also a thick paperback book with a crinkled cover and curled pages that looked as if it had been passed around for the entire island to read.

"Five minutes I'll be through with this part and you can jump in." He pushed a piece of spiral hose with his foot. "Once I backwash the filter, that's it."

Dallas saw that the door to the sun room was open. The placid surface of the hot tub steamed with heat. "You sure no one's home?"

"Nobody here but us chickens." Adam saw Dallas walking toward the door. "I've got a key to turn off the alarm. The backyard's on a motion detector. Sounds an alarm to keep people from pool hopping."

The smell of chlorine was potent from the hot tub as Dallas poked his head in, looked through another opened door into the living room. Pale gray carpet had been freshly vacuumed and cushy furniture rearranged into two clustered seating areas.

"You live down here all year?" Dallas asked Adam. Fifteen years ago, he would have known the answer just by looking at him, but that was when the year-round population was 1,500, not 30,000.

"Go to school at Washington University."

"Where's that?"

"St. Louis."

Dallas strolled away from the house, looked at the pool. The white bottom appeared spotless, but Adam kept vacuuming prodigiously nonetheless. If the Ocean Tides ever installed a pool — yeah, right — Dallas would have to offer him a job. "You're — what — a junior?"

"Senior. This is it, man. Last year."

"Congratulations."

"Then off to Wall Street."

"Stockbroker?"

"No way. Banker."

"So this is the last honest job you'll have."

"Hey!" the kid protested, but wasn't really upset. "I'm gonna be bustin' my ass up there. You make a couple hundred G's in New York, you're in the big leagues."

Dallas wondered if he should hook Adam up with Teresa Jane.

"Not that I'm money hungry — "

"Of course not." Dallas flourished when it came to sarcasm.

"You know," Adam defended himself, "it's a fact of our age — my — age — that the American dream of living a better life than your parents is no longer a sure thing. In fact, odds are most people going into the work force in the next five years will be working harder than their parents, but won't achieve the same life-style."

Adam rested the vacuum pole on his bare shoulder, needing his hands for emphasis as he went on with what sounded to Dallas like a regurgitation of some Economy 101 professor's pep talk for greed. Adam's eyes sparkled with an almost religious fervor. "Because more people are now living at a higher level than ever means it gets harder and harder for the next generation to climb the ladder to the next rung. It can only go so far, you know. The American Dream, hey, it's going to plateau out. Which wouldn't be bad, I guess." Adam shrugged, not seeming at all convinced. "But, the way it is, you don't do better than your old man, you're a failure." That, he seemed to believe whole-heartedly. "So you do what it takes."

"That's why you're going into banking?"

"I wanna retire by the time I'm twenty-five. Thirty, tops." He winked, college cocky, probably never having been exposed to enough reality to know how rough the competition was — or how ruthless. "My own problem is I got this ROTC commitment. The U.S.A.'s been footing my tuition at Wash U. and now it's payback time. Talk about a bitch. But I think I got an angle. These stock market high rollers I know in the Big Apple? They think they can get me out of it. Money talks, you know. It can be done. Watch out for Number One."

Dallas felt embarrassed for the kid. Dallas didn't know much about New York or banking, except that there was probably a hungry swarm of financial sharks waiting up there to have a feeding frenzy on naïve rookies like Adam. Dallas pictured some big yuk in a gray flannel suit picking up Adam by his ankles, sticking him headfirst down his gizzard, then pulling him out clean, nothing left but bones he'd snap off for toothpicks.

Dallas took a seat on the diving board. "You know Jud Fitch?"

"Jud. Yeah, sure. He's a money mover, too. Might be competing with me for a job some day."

"I don't think so." Dallas squinted into the sun. "Jud's dead. He fell off a high-rise balcony last Friday."

"Oh, shit . . . Man, you're kidding? Jud?" When Dallas nodded, Adam exhaled deeply, as if the wind had been knocked out of him. *Damn.* Man, you never know." He stared into the silky water as he vacuumed another swipe across the already clean bottom. "Suicide, huh?"

"Was Jud the type to kill himself?"

"I don't know any of us that doesn't think about it. I know three kids who ended it in high school, three more in college. You know, like Jim Morrison."

"Did Jud ever talk about it with you?"

"I probably wouldn't remember if he had. It would have been a nonevent. You know . . . talk."

What the hell was it with these kids? Dallas wondered. Wasn't there any subject they didn't take nonchalantly? Drugs. Money. Suicide. Dallas shook the thought out of his head; he was thinking like an old guy, an old *worried* guy. If he didn't watch it, he might be mistaken for someone's father again.

"You know," Dallas said, "Jud came into a lot of money lately. Selling drugs has been mentioned as a possibility more than once."

"Not Jud Fitch. No way. He was clean." Adam wiped his face with what Dallas had first thought to be a T-shirt, but was actually a large kerchief. "He must've gotten the money from his old man."

"I don't think so."

"Why? How much're you talking about?"

Dallas wasn't sure if Adam seemed jealous or curious. "More than gas money."

Adam thought about that, then shook his head. "Nah. His old man gave it to him."

Dallas didn't press the point. "You know who Jud hung around with? I've got this list." He took the napkin from his shorts pocket and unfolded it. The soft paper was beginning to fall apart from abuse, but the names Terry had written were still legible.

"Lemme see." Adam tossed aside his sweat rag.

"How about someone named Polo?"

"Polo? Where'd you hear that?"

"Some girl said Jud had been hanging around with him. She said Polo owned this house. An old guy who's supposed to like boys."

Adam laughed long and hard. "That's ripe. That's really ripe."

Dallas figured it was an inside joke.

$\triangledown$

1 7

THE BIG KID WITH the military-recruit haircut did a reverse dunk with such authority the entire recreation park trembled. As his $150 high-tops landed feather-soft on the outdoor court, he announced, "Game," without the slightest hint of conceit.

The loser didn't mind paying up. He seemed thankful to have survived and was probably wondering how he thought he could have beaten the moose in the first place. Sometimes cocky was good. Other times it cost money. In this case, though, not much.

The loser's bushy red hair was matted to his forehead with sweat. He dug into the pockets of tight shorts imprinted with a Roanoke College logo and came out with crumpled dollar bills. The money was soaking wet and caked with bits of sand from an earlier swim in the ocean. Beach money.

When he handed the big kid in the Mt. Hebron game jersey a five spot, the giant neatly brushed it from his palm like a tiger shooing away an annoying cub.

"Nice game." The winner had an easy, unassuming smile.

Dallas had arrived when the game was tied 5–5, then witnessed the big kid, Kurt, run off six straight make-it-take-it hoops, finishing off with the monster dunk.

At six-foot-five, 240 pounds, Kurt had more of a football player's build but was surprisingly agile. His massive thighs were spring-loaded with enough velocity for his forearms to amply clear the rim of the ten-foot hoop.

The scary thing was, another spectator told Dallas Kurt was only seventeen. If that was true, Dallas figured he'd probably been getting served in bars since he was twelve. Put Kurt undercover with the liquor board cops, they'd close up the entire town for underage violations in one night.

"You set for a breather?" Dallas asked, approaching the court Kurt seemed to own.

"You like to play?" Kurt had such a gentle voice Dallas wasn't offended that his idea of a breather would be to play him one-on-one. Despite the heat and humidity of late afternoon, Kurt didn't seem the least drained by his efforts.

"You know Terry?" Dallas asked. "I'm not sure of her last name, but she said you knew Jud Fitch."

"Sure." Kurt tucked the orange ball under his arm and wiped his face with black-and-orange wrist bands. "He was a pretty nice guy. I was sorry to hear what happened to him."

Dallas thought this wasn't fair. Was this kid going to be that big and compassionate, too? Women loved that kind of guy. Dallas was jealous as hell. He even found himself sucking in his stomach to pretend he was fit. "If you got a minute, I'm trying to find out some things about Jud . . . for his family."

"Yeah, that'd be fine. Boy, that's terrible something like that happens. Must be really hard on his folks." As Kurt walked off the court, five other players tentatively edged to where he'd been playing.

"Okay if we shoot around, Kurt?" one asked.

Kurt said, "Sure," like, why were they asking him.

Kurt and Dallas sat front row on aluminum benches. The courts were enclosed by a fifteen-foot chain fence designed to keep balls from bouncing out into traffic.

The park covered a four-block area and included two softball fields. This was the sportsman's battleground where local businesses sent their more athletic employees to quest after coveted basketball and softball league trophies each summer.

As Dallas and Kurt talked, rows of sprinklers danced to life over the dusty ball fields behind them. Little kids wearing Orioles batting helmets screamed happily running the bases between sprays of cool water.

Going into details about Jud, Kurt's conversation pretty well reiterated what Dallas already knew, until the name Polo came up.

"I don't know who he is," Kurt said, "but he must be some kind of guy." Kurt rested his elbows on his knees, watching the basketball

98

courts as if already missed playing. "Jud was ape over him. It was like he'd found a hero or something." Kurt spoke well, as though tendering answers to an oral history final. "It's sort of hard to describe."

"Do you know what he looks like? Polo?"

"He didn't hang around with us, and Jud was usually pretty secretive about what he and Polo were doing. It was like he didn't want anyone to know, but on the other hand, was dying to tell someone."

"Did Jud ever show any . . ." Dallas hesitated posing the question, ". . . homosexual tendencies?"

Kurt's lips curled with momentary consideration, his mouth making a slight humming sound before finally coming out with a denial. "I don't think so. Nothing I ever saw, but who would he tell about that?"

Dallas nodded.

Kurt wiped a bead of sweat from his eye. "I guess he was having a good time, but once Jud started hanging out with Polo he left the rest of us in the dust. Couple weeks ago, back in June, I really busted my ass to get him a ticket to Robert Plant. We were all driving up to Merriweather in Jake's van, then coming back the same night 'cause some people had to work Sunday. Jud had been on me to get him that ticket, which I finally got from this scalper for fifty bucks. Night of the concert" — Kurt turned up his palms — "no Jud. Later, he said he was sorry for being a no-show, said something about Polo, but you would have thought he'd at least offer to cover the ticket." Kurt shook his head. "No way."

As Dallas drove out of the lot, the descending sun cast a deep orange haze and long shadows over the old clapboard buildings that surrounded the rec center.

A girl on Terry's list named Jeannie Hall — someone who'd dated Jud recently — shared an apartment a few blocks from the downtown bridge. Dallas found the address easily enough.

Within a good third-baseman's throw of Assawoman Bay, the wood-planked two-story appeared in lopsided juxtaposition to the level horizon; the little gray apartment house seemed to list easily on its starboard side, like an injured boat taking on more water than its bilge could expel.

The fatigued house carried a tired history that marked a survival of high tides and swollen seas like hash marks of victory proudly inscribed on a fighter pilot's fuselage. Even the air smelled rich with salt water, as though the house emitted the aroma as its own.

Breathing deeply of creosote-stained bulkheads, Dallas stepped onto a cracked walkway and aimed his way toward the door.

A slender girl with dark free-flowing hair took three steps from the house, then stopped abruptly at the sight of him. Her easy gait froze as a hint of what Dallas perceived as panic widened her eyes.

"Didn't mean to startle you." Dallas smiled.

She backed toward the house, glancing over her shoulder. It was as if he was someone's father paying a surprise visit and she couldn't remember if they'd stashed the Coors and condoms.

"I'm looking for Jeannie Hall? I'd like to talk to her about Jud Fitch."

The girl stopped short of the front step. "She's not here." Her voice was neither steady nor convincing, but her posture seemed to draw a line of defense she didn't want Dallas to cross.

He didn't.

A young woman in an oversized T-shirt watched from inside the house. Her long hair laid over the arm she braced against the screen door.

"Jeannie?" Dallas asked.

"I told you she's not here," the girl in front of him repeated.

"She's not here," the one inside confirmed, her tone more definite, more we-don't-take-any-crap than her counterpart.

"I'm just trying to find out some things about Judson Fitch. I thought Jeannie could help."

"She's not here." The sentry inside the door opened the screen for her friend to complete her withdrawal into the house.

"So you said." Dallas wasn't used to encountering this degree of paranoia. After all, it was the beach. Everyone was supposed to leave that psychological mess on the other side of the bridge. "If you see her, ask her to call Dallas Henry. That's me. I'm at the Ocean Tides Motel. Okay?" He tried to see through the darkening screen, hoping for some sign of acknowledgment. "Ocean Tides Motel. Dallas Henry. Tell her, okay?"

She closed the door.

Left standing there, Dallas figured he now knew what it felt like to sell subscriptions of *The Watchtower* door to door.

It took Dallas twenty minutes to drive fifteen blocks to the end of the boardwalk. The evening traffic rush had snarled the only possible route.

The packed grid of traffic reminded Dallas of an old Jimmy Walker joke: a guy waiting in the unemployment line is complaining, "Hey, this line's not moving," to which another guy answers, "No shit, if it was moving it'd be a parade."

When Dallas finally reached the inlet parking lot, the Lord of Crowds was on his side. He got a space close to the amusement pier just as a van of West Virginia fun boys pulled out. They even left him time on the meter.

Dallas plunked in a few more quarters to be on the safe side, then risked his life crossing the lot.

Grits driving Trans Ams overrevved their powerful engines. These would-be studlies were after the cheap cuties who wore outdated halter tops and had butterfly tattoos on their butts.

Dallas swore some of them were the same kids he'd seen hanging out on Ninth Street dressed in beads and hip-hugger bell-bottoms during the late sixties.

On the boardwalk, the eateries were all packed with families struggling to keep their kids' attention long enough to force-feed them fried chicken and french fries before hitting the arcades.

One nine-year-old boy with flyaway blond hair had a good argument for passing dinner. "I'm just gonna boof it once I get off the twist-a-whirl anyway."

Dallas eased into the flow of pedestrian traffic and tried not to get sucked into the building where horns and sirens blasted from Trimper's kiddy rides.

At the Inlet Park, the line to buy roller coaster tickets coiled down the block like a multiheaded snake.

"Bobby," Dallas called to the guy running the speed ball booth. "How's it goin'?"

"Like shit. These kids're driving me crazy."

The park was wild, crowded and loud with tourists. A little girl with a mountain of cotton candy plowed into the back of her father's stretch-knit pants. The disc jockey running the Matterhorn ride screamed over stereo speakers, asking if everyone wanted to go Faaaasssssster!

"Goddamn tourists go home!" Bobby yelled at people waiting in line at his amusement.

Two sets of parents guided their children away, saying the radar gun was rigged anyway and that the kiddy bumper cars were better.

"Hey!" Bobby yelled at a kid trying to sneak an extra ball. "You do that one more time and that's it. I'll smash you. You're nothing. I'll crush you under my thumb."

101

"I'm gonna play," the kid whined, not threatened in the least.

"Like hell. Not till you gimme another dollar." Bobby barked orders from beneath the tilted brim of a Chicago Cubs batting helmet three sizes too small.

The kid obliged and Bobby angrily kicked three rubber balls toward him. "And don't step over the line, goddamnit."

Another set of parents eased their daughter over to the House of Mirrors.

"Miserable little bastards," Bobby swore under his breath. On his ripped white T-shirt was an iron-on of a homicidal surfer and the slogan, I'M A LOCAL ANYWHERE.

The kid wound up pretty good and threw his first ball dead center in the strike zone, lighting 45 on the radar gun board.

"Forty-five," Bobby announced without enthusiasm.

"I can read," the kid said.

"Yeah, not when I pluck out your eyes you can't." Bobby flexed the muscles he'd been working on in the Sheraton gym. "Go over that line again you'll be learning braille. Try getting through *Moby Dick* in freshman English using your fingers, peckerhead."

On the next ball, the kid reached back and put his shoulder into it.

"Forty-nine for the kid who wants to get his eyes popped out."

The line of youngsters waiting their turn to throw was diminishing in a hurry; some grandmother type muttered about complaining to the management.

"How long you been at this, Bobby?" Dallas asked.

"Half hour."

"I don't think you're gonna last."

Bobby grabbed the kid's arm before he threw his last ball. "Make a guess, kid. How fast you gonna throw?"

"Fifty-five."

"Bullshit. Bet you ten bucks you can't top fifty."

The kid grinned and threw it fifty-six miles per hour.

Bobby flicked back the brim of his cap. "I don't believe it. A speed-ball shark."

"Pay up, mister."

"Here." Bobby dumped over a box full of balls. "On the house. I hope your rag-ass arm falls off."

"Good pitcher," Dallas said.

"Gun must be broken. I threw here all night last week, couldn't break forty-three. Cost me twenty bucks."

Dallas backed him away from the speed-ball cage, having to speak up as loud music and screams from the Matterhorn ride increased, kids getting twirled backward at nauseating speeds. "You ever heard of a guy named Polo?"

"What is this, World History? I'm on summer break."

"A local, maybe? Someone around here goes by Polo? Maybe a queer who owns property in Rehobeth?"

Bobby got defensive. "I don't hang out with faggots."

"He might not be. I just heard a name, I'd like to know who it goes to."

"I can ask around."

Behind Bobby's back, the kid was selling three throws at the speed-ball booth for a dollar and pocketing the proceeds.

Dallas said, "Call me if something comes up."

"Sure, yeah. Okay." Bobby started to turn away, then snapped his fingers and waved Dallas back. "You got another one of your business cards? I gave my last one to some guy last week. Jud Fitch. He ever call you?"

18

"WHAT'RE YOU DOING HERE? Nobody's watching the desk." Comfortable on one of the double beds in the motel room Dallas called home, Herbie was watching TV. He had his head propped up by two fluffy pillows. "It's a wildcat strike. My lawyer'll be calling you as soon as he gets out of jail to renegotiate my contract."

"Swell." Dallas grabbed a mostly empty bottle of peach wine cooler from the refrigerator. He hated that particular flavor, but was thirsty. How could the young girls he brought back to his place like it so much? They said it was smooooooth. "Hey, Herbie. You ever heard of a guy named Polo?"

"You're doing it wrong," Herbie said. "You're supposed to give *me* the answer and *I* say the question."

Dallas looked at the color TV — well, the images were in *some* color, not necessarily human. "Jeopardy" was on. Some guy named Chuck was going through the Battles of Charlemagne category like a spear into Medieval butter, racking up points.

"Okay," Dallas told Herbie, "the category is Ocean City Notables. For a thousand bucks, the answer is Polo."

On TV, Chuck took Biblical Emperors for $400.

"The answer is Polo . . ." Herbie mulled that over. "I got it. What's a silly-assed game where guys ride horses and bang a little white ball with sticks?"

"Wrong." Dallas did the best Alex Trebek he could manage. "Remember the category: Ocean City Notables."

104

Herbie twisted long strands of blond hair and pondered further.

Chuck hit the Daily Double on Biblical Emperors for $800, bet five grand and got it right. The audience went wild. Alex Trebek glanced off-stage toward Merv Griffin to see if they had enough money in the checkbook.

Herbie guessed, "What's a brand of overpriced shirts with emblems of men on horseback playing a silly-assed game?"

"Wrong again." Leaning against the kitchenette table, Dallas saw a pot in the sink caked irreversibly with bits of hamburger and fried onions. "How long've you been here?"

"What's, since five o'clock?" Herbie answered "Jeopardy"-style.

Dallas tried to clean cooked-on grime from the skillet, but only managed to disembowel an SOS pad. "You better get some dynamite and clean this mess up."

"Can't." Herbie hopped off the bed. He left the TV on and headed toward the Ocean Tides office.

"Why not?"

"I'm on the desk."

Dallas grabbed Herbie's skinny arm as he went by. "You clean. I'll cover till you're done."

Dallas picked up the call on the ancient switchboard without noticing the originating room. "Front desk."

The voice on the other end said, "Oh," sounding surprised. "I was expecting Herbie." It was Teresa Jane.

"Don't be silly. What would he be doing working?" Strange, but Dallas was glad to hear her voice. "You need something? More aspirin?"

"Don't remind me." She feigned pain, but he could hear her smiling. "I was calling to find out if you were back yet. And . . . there you are." Her tone was flush with a subdued enthusiasm that was going to start sounding happy if she didn't watch it. "I'm sorry about last night. That was a real first for me."

"Don't worry about it. It's the beach." Dallas absently glanced through the phone messages. Two from the hotel's accountant he crumpled up and tossed into the trash can.

"I guess . . . actually," Teresa Jane said, "I should be thanking you."

"For what? You paid for dinner. I didn't do anything."

She paused. "That's why I'm thanking you."

"Oh." Dallas caught the innuendo like a line drive smacked into the webbing of a fielder's mitt. "That's a funny thing about me, I guess. I like women all ages, shapes, sizes. Dumb ones. Smart ones. Girls who have great tans . . . those who don't. But I definitely like them sober."

"How gallant."

"Nah. It's an ego thing. I'm at that age where I like to think whoever I'm with is into me, not a bottle of Seagrams. . . . Unless, of course," Dallas qualified, "she's really hot and there's no other way."

Teresa Jane laughed, then proposed that they try dinner again.

"My treat," Dallas insisted.

Dallas held the bucket of Popeye's chicken under one arm and opened the door to Teresa Jane's room with the other. "As you can see, traffic, not food preparation, was what took so long."

Teresa Jane turned off the TV, what looked to have been — could it have been? — a quasi-smut movie on one of the pay stations. What, no public broadcasting talk show? No "Master Bore Theatre"?

"Something smells very enticing," Dallas complimented her sincerely, "and it's not the chicken."

Teresa Jane glanced over her shoulder as she led the way to the balcony. "You like it? It's an after-bath splash. Susan picked it out."

Dallas was intrigued. The scent was evocative, just subtle hints of it seducing his olfactories like peaks of lean legs from beneath long skirts with high slits. He wondered if Susan had also selected Teresa Jane's attire.

She wore an emerald-green silk pullover with a wide neckline that caressed her shoulders like a soft cloud. The top stopped just short of the waist of a hip-tight skirt; a skirt that zipped down the back, which Dallas always found enticing.

Teresa Jane started to slide open the screen door, but it stuck. "I've been having a little trouble with this."

"Kick it," Dallas instructed. "Right along the bottom ledge."

Barefooted, Teresa Jane tapped it with the side of her foot.

"No. *Kick*." Dallas thumped it hard with the toe of his Nikes and the screen popped back into its salt-encrusted track. He gestured with the barrel of chicken that she should go out first.

"Why, thank you." Teresa used the same proper tone with which she addressed New York City doormen.

"You betcha, toots."

Teresa Jane had made up the small plastic table with what she had to work with. One of her business-mode skirts was the tablecloth, which left an uncovered hole in the middle that was filled nicely by the

Popeye's bucket. Emergency votive candles — stocked in each hotel room per safety code — were placed in plain water glasses, which were then filled with an inch of sparkling Cherry 7-Up. When lit, the candles appeared to flicker on a lake of amethysts.

"Very nice," Dallas said admiringly, then glanced at what was decoratively wrapped around the balcony railing.

"Toilet paper," Teresa Jane confirmed with an ingenious nod. "There wasn't any crepe."

"You're catching on to Ocean City life." Dallas sat down and pried the lid off the chicken.

Teresa Jane retrieved two bottles of Bartles and James Berry from a Styrofoam chest packed with hotel ice. In the candlelight, her hair took on the warm silky glow of amber.

There weren't any plates, just paper towels, so Dallas laid a spicy thigh in front of Teresa Jane, not hesitating to put it directly on her skirt/tablecloth.

She didn't seem to mind.

"We also have cole slaw," Dallas said, digging around in the big bucket, "red beans and rice, biscuits and honey, and jalapeño peppers."

"Sounds good. I'm starved." Teresa Jane even unscrewed the caps to the wine coolers and drank straight from the bottle.

Three stories below them, the evening's first wave of vacationers strolled back from a night in boomtown. Little kids were zonked out in squeaky-wheel strollers that bounced over uneven slats of boardwalk. With their toddlers out of it, Mom and Dad were left to haul a small menagerie of stuffed animals and claw-machine prizes under their arms.

On the beach, bright green light sticks were tossed into the dark sky by three nine-year-olds. As the glowing cylinders fell back to the sand, the boys dove with overly dramatic enthusiasm trying to catch them. When their parents called out from half a block farther on, the kids hustled to catch up, then began to throw their new toys skyward again.

"They never seem to run out of energy, do they?" Teresa Jane asked. She peered beneath the top railing to watch the boys with the glow sticks.

Dallas watched them, too, turning in his seat with a chicken leg in his fingers. "It's been so long since I was that age . . ."

"You sound like you miss it."

Dallas nodded. "I do. Things were so much simpler. And the stuff I was afraid of . . . hell . . . monsters under the bed, Martians with five heads, the basement . . . it wasn't even real." He chewed a bite of chicken. "*That* is the real beauty of that age. Well, two things, I guess. You're never short of breath and you haven't found out all there really is to be afraid of yet."

The boys and their illuminated toys grew distant as they hurried along after their parents, always a few paces behind. Trying to act independent without straying too far off.

"Do you know what I was afraid of?" Teresa Jane asked.

"I don't know. . . . Bogeymen?"

"Failure."

Dallas laughed, but he didn't really find it funny. "Hell, then you didn't even have a childhood."

"Sometimes I don't think so. But it never seemed to matter. I always liked adult things. Most of my friends were older kids, so I tried to act like them."

Dallas felt around in the bucket for the jalapeño peppers. "What were you going to fail at?"

"I never wanted to disappoint my parents."

"Forget that. Disappointing parents is what being a kid's all about. It's what being a son or daughter is about. Forever. It never ends. You just get old enough, then you don't live with them anymore. The disapproval becomes distant enough everyone can pretend it doesn't exist."

Dallas took a healthy bite of jalapeño, waited until it got his mouth and lips hot, then guzzled wine cooler. "Ahhh." He plopped down the bottle. "But you can't blame parents. They've got lots of time, a scary amount of bucks invested in a kid, so it's hard not to feel betrayed when they sneak out with the family car before they're old enough to drive. Smoke dope, play hookie. Marry too young, *and* someone not good enough. Get a job that's a little below their qualifications, then have kids of their own that they raise *all* wrong." Dallas ate red beans and rice straight from the container with a bent Ocean Tides el-cheapo fork.

Teresa Jane reached for another piece of chicken with greasy fingers. "So what's the Dallas Henry patented cure for the woes of the world?"

"I'm not sure there is one," he answered, chewing. "But, I guess, in theory, you live at the beach. Where it's warm. Drink. And don't have kids."

Teresa Jane looked toward the ocean, where the moon was beginning to rise big and orange above the endless dark blue horizon. "I think, sometimes, that my father wishes he hadn't had children. I think we've both disappointed him. Jud sure has." She slowly took apart a piece of chicken laid across her tablecloth-fashioned skirt. "And I guess I'm here trying not to feel guilty about having a good time."

"Because of Jud?"

"I don't know what happened to him, Dallas. I really don't. It was like I knew him, but I didn't. Looking back on it, it's as if he were a complete stranger." She was eating the chicken, but didn't seem to taste it, as though her thoughts made the motion automatic. "I think, maybe, it was all a front. That the last couple years when I saw him he put on a 'family' face — that kind of everything's-rosy attitude you manage for holidays and reunions — when, deep down, he must have been very troubled."

Dallas wasn't so sure about that, but didn't offer any argument. He sensed that even though Teresa Jane was talking about her brother, she was really talking about herself, *and* her father. And he didn't know why, but this didn't seem to be the right time to tell her someone had seen her father in Ocean City with Jud. Dallas sensed that it would be traumatic, that it would push Teresa Jane back toward her prim and proper ways, and he didn't want that to happen.

There was a brief silence, both of them eating more slowly now that the initial ravages of hunger had been warded off.

Wiping her hands to open a second wine cooler for herself, Teresa Jane said, "Do you know this is the first vacation I've had since I graduated from high school? That summer, my father agreed to pay my way to Europe with a group from school. God, I had a great time. We were in London and Paris. The Greek islands. It was incredible.

"But after that, every summer I spent working intern jobs in banks or investment firms. They were grueling hours. Those guys loved having college kids to torture with inane chores they pretended were work. And I think the fact that I was one of the few females really turned some of them on. Ordering me around through bullwork deals got their rocks off. They'd hand me mile-long spread sheets of data and want all sorts of bizarre correlations that never came to anything."

Teresa Jane tried some of the cole slaw. "Mmm, vinegary." She took another bite. "When I was stuck in those intern jobs, I used to complain about it to my father — I think I was really throwing hints, hoping he'd spring for another trip, but no way. He told me to tough it out. I had to pay my dues. There would be great jobs waiting once I graduated that other kids would have to fight years to get."

Teresa Jane stared at the table, suddenly absorbed by the memory. "And he was right. I got a great job. Right out of college. Twenty-two years old, I was making eighty-nine-five with bonuses and stock options that netted over a hundred grand. And the investment angles I saw added another ten percent on top of that. Because I was making way more than I was spending. And because I had the discipline to look into it. I'd go to bed early even on Friday and Saturday nights so that I didn't throw off the routine and wake up groggy Monday morning. I was good at that life." She broke her stare and looked right at Dallas. "I *am* good at it."

Dallas nodded in agreement. "I bet you kick their asses."

She seemed surprised to hear someone actually compliment her. "I'm not the best, I'm not perfect, but I'm good." It was as if she wanted to see whether that qualification would make him withdraw his words of praise, which he didn't.

"So how come," Teresa Jane proposed, "Some nights I wake up at three A.M. scared to death? How come slow songs make me cry? How come I can go on Valium binges that barely take the edge off?"

"How come," Dallas countered, "you still like to be called T.J.?"

Once their joint effort had dinner cleaned up, leftovers stashed in the refrigerator, Dallas proposed a walk on the beach and T.J. — as he was now calling her — agreed.

She said he should go ahead, that she'd meet him down there, and when she arrived at the lifeguard stand fifteen minutes later, Dallas felt an incredible surge press through him.

T.J. still wore the tight skirt, but her hair was loose, no longer confined in a tortoiseshell barrette. And, she'd changed into Susan's white blouse, the one that was Dallas's favorite. The one with the lace cuffs and frilly collar that buttoned all the way to her throat, and was the hottest thing Dallas had ever seen coming or going.

T.J. even looked better in it than Susan somehow. Or maybe it was the glow of the moonlight. Or the way she held his hand. Or the fact that she wasn't wearing anything beneath it.

No words were spoken. Yet, in the silence was understanding as they walked north along the shoreline, looking for a dark stretch of dunes, where the sand was soft and warm, night air rustled the sea grass, and buttons came undone amidst passionate sighs of desire.

$\triangledown$

19

SUSAN WOULDN'T SO MUCH as say good morning. She didn't want to have to undo her gloating smile as she worked efficiently on the reservations board.

"Stop humming!" Dallas shouted cheerfully from his office, where he was going through Jud's papers, looking for that Bethany Beach phone number.

Susan deliberately hummed louder. Then, unable to hold back any longer, she strolled into his office, leaned over Dallas's desk with an I-know-what-you've-been-up-to-grin. "Tell me," she bragged, curling dark hair framing her pretty face and bright eyes, "that I'm not the greatest matchmaker of all times. *Tell me*, that I didn't call it from the first day she set foot in this place."

Dallas leaned back in his chair. It was actually a few minutes before noon and he felt nicely awake. "I had a good time with her last night," he admitted. "A real good time. Does that make you happy?"

Susan gave out a quick cry of victory.

Dallas tossed Jud's phone bill into the center of his desk, having circled the calls to the Bethany Beach number. "If you're so great, how about finding the street address that goes to that?"

"Forty bucks?" Dallas didn't think he had that much money on him. "I thought we ordered flowers, not gold bullion."

"So's your ass." Jack carefully set eighteen deep red roses next to the cash register.

Jack Brittingham had wavy salt-and-pepper hair that was kinked irreparably from summer humidity. His narrow shoulders were hunched from spending too much time bent over what always turned out to be incredible bouquets of freshly cut blossoms. Outstanding work was what saved his business from being spoiled by what most people considered a strangely gruff attitude for a florist.

Jack's temperament was more suited to working a deli counter. He liked to say, "So's your ass," whenever he had the chance. It was his own interpretation on the more philosophical, "That's life," or the benign, "Have a nice day."

Dallas peeled open the Velcro seam of his wallet. How unusual, he didn't have any money. "Can you bill me for this? Come to think of it, bill the hotel. I'll tell the accountant it was for a replacement door. He'll complain I paid too much, but I'll hang up on him."

"Yup." Jack made a notation on the pink invoice.

"Thanks for the robbery, Jack," Dallas said, jingling the miniature cow bells attached to the door on his way out.

"So's your ass," Jack said, waving.

Sea Knoll Court was a surprisingly private road for the beach front. Dallas had passed it hundreds of times over the years before realizing it was even there.

The court was lined by a stand of twenty-foot white pines. Its access from the main highway was a gravel apron marked PRIVATE. There wasn't even the usual government-issue street sign, just a decorative wood plaque mounted to a cornerstone, engraved SEA KNOLL COURT. The setting bespoke wealthy seclusion, where the haves sought refuge from have-nots like Dallas.

The architecture was mostly mid-seventies modern. Lots of flat roofs tilted at varying pitches over tall, narrow windows. Every home was well maintained and sported some type of recent addition designed to make the look more current.

In the driveway of one of the larger homes, a teenaged girl with a trendy haircut and killer body eyed Dallas's rusty 280 suspiciously as he cruised by. She threw her beach bag into a fire engine red Mercedes convertible, but waited until Dallas was out of sight to get into the car, acting as if he'd been watching her undress.

The house Dallas was after sat back off the cul-de-sac end of Sea Knoll Court. A brick driveway lined with stove-black "waterfront" pole lamps led to a three-story contemporary built just west of the dune line.

"So's your ass, Jack," Dallas mumbled making a drive by. This was the address that corresponded to the Bethany Beach number on Jud's phone bill. And Dallas thought the bayside party house had set the owner back some bucks. That was a thirty percent down payment on this place.

It was by far the biggest home on the road. No contest. Designed, without doubt, by some high-priced architect who'd managed to get the most house on a narrow-but-deep lot.

Washed brick the color of a desert sunset faced the lower half of the house, then gave way to wide-lipped sand-colored siding up to a slate roof. Arched windows and orange-slice vents dotted the exterior like perfectly placed diamonds on a solid gold setting.

When Dallas parked one house away and turned off the engine, he heard waves breaking beyond the dunes. The sound of his Nikes on loose gravel was surprisingly audible along with the gently swaying branches of white pines moved by the breeze. If the intent of those living on this court was to block out the rest of the world, they'd done one hell of a job.

As soon as Dallas walked within sight of the huge beach house, he quickened his gait to seem more efficient. Roses in one hand, he went up the slanted driveway, glancing at his mock delivery schedule.

Susan had conned this address from the woman who'd answered the phone. Claiming to be a dispatcher from FTD, Susan said they had a delivery of fresh flowers, but everything on the ticket had smeared except the phone number of the addressee. The woman had willingly given her address *complete with directions*. Susan, once again victorious, had told Dallas, "I don't think I could be any more perfect, do you?"

On the front door was a grapevine wreath adorned with blue bows and tiny conch shells. When Dallas rang the bell, it chimed as though peacefully summoning a convent of nuns from afternoon meditation.

Dallas figured, if ever someone was going to be seduced by money, this place would do it. So maybe Jud Fitch had met the daughter of whoever lived here and needed to keep-up-with-the-Rockefellers to impress her. That would explain why selling drugs had suddenly become a good idea, assuming that's what he'd been doing.

The door was opened by a stunning woman Dallas guessed was in her early forties. She wore a pale pink silk robe that clung to moist, bronzed flesh. Her loosely curled hair was long and thick and damp at the ends as though she'd just gotten out of the tub.

113

Good God was all Dallas could manage to think.

Her makeup was subtle. Hints of peach-chocolate eye shadow made pale green eyes glow seductively. Fire-coral lip gloss glistened like sticky ice cream across a sensual, wide mouth. "They're very pretty," the woman said.

Dallas had no idea what she was talking about. Then remembered as she took them from him — oh, yeah, the flowers. Barefoot, she set them beside a stack of mail on a polished Chippendale writing table.

The foyer had a marble floor. Overhead, a small chandelier cast sparkly reflections against glossy rose walls.

"Do I need to sign anything?" She glanced at his clipboard.

Dallas didn't want to think, didn't want to interrupt the fantasies her sexily unassuming voice had inspired in him. But he forced himself. Discipline, after all, was his middle name. "Yeah, uh, this." Smiling stupidly, he held out the clipboard, then felt his shirt pocket "Shoot. Can you wait a second? I must've dropped my pen on the way in." He turned to start back down the driveway.

"I have one here," she volunteered.

Dallas turned around in time to see her bending over the Chippendale. He only wished the drawer were a little lower, because if she tilted forward a tad more, her breasts were going to fall out of that robe. And something about cheap thrills and rich women was such fun.

"Felt tip okay?" she asked, finding one.

"Oh yeah." Dallas half swooned.

She made an inconsequential adjustment to her robe and stood upright.

Dallas turned the clipboard around, directing her to the first unused line below where Susan had scribbled a smorgasbord of fake signatures.

The woman gave Dallas a cordial smile while signing the form. "Thanks again," she said. "They really are beautiful." Then, misinterpreting his infatuation as a hint for a tip, she said, "Wait a moment, will you?"

Dallas started to stop her, but began enjoying the view of her hurrying down the hall. That robe wasn't nearly as long as he'd first thought. She disappeared from view, rooting around for loose change.

Dallas glanced around the foyer, up the long staircase to the second floor, thinking there should have been a sign, NIRVANA THIS WAY. Then he looked at his phonied delivery form, where she'd signed her name. Olivia Miles.

And then realized, Uh-oh. Her handwriting matched that of the *Dear Judson* letter. A fact that was confirmed when she returned with two bucks for his tip, then asked if he'd mind putting her mail out in the box.

All the envelopes were in the same style of writing. But, just to make sure, Dallas stole them.

2 0

"**Y**OU KNOW DIVERTING MAIL is a federal offense."

"Ah, they don't even know where Ocean City is," Dallas told Susan, reiterating the doper's line from the party house as he carefully slit open the first envelope. The *Dear Jud* letter was already on his blotter, awaiting confirmation. "Check this out," Dallas invited, unfolding the stolen letter next to the other. "You're so perfect today. You call that a match?"

The "borrowed" letter was a short note to some aunt in North Carolina, Olivia Miles writing that she hoped she was feeling better. The note also said that she — Olivia — was doing much better these days herself. Dallas guessed so, in that house, with that body, how could she miss?

Susan stood close beside Dallas, but he was too distracted by his find to pay her his usual grab-ass due.

"Where did you get this one?" she asked of the *Dear Jud*, reading it.

"The kid's condo."

"My, my, this is steamy. Looks like there was a little summer romance going here."

"And I thought he was chasing her daughter. I'm gonna have to start giving this kid more credit." Dallas leaned back. "I mean how do you meet women like that?"

" 'You knew the limits of my affections,' " Susan read. " 'You knew that certain things could never be.' I wonder what she meant by that?"

"Who knows? Maybe he wanted to tie her up with suede belts and smear Cool Whip all over her body."

"Ohhw, fun!"

"Don't tempt me," Dallas warned.

Susan gave him that go-ahead look, the one they always played around with that never came to anything. Then she went back to the letter. " '. . . We simply cannot continue to see each other. It would only lead . . . to something very foolish that we might each well live to regret." Susan paused. "Live to regret? Sounds a little heavy-duty doesn't it?"

"Wait a minute," Dallas thought, sitting up, grabbing the phone bill. "I mean it's obvious, right? She's married. Look at this. All these phone calls Jud made to her place that got billed at the three-minute minimum."

"If a man answers, hang up," Susan said.

"You got it."

"You think," Susan said, "maybe her husband found out . . ."

"Decided to give Jud a push off a balcony," Dallas said, finishing her thought. "Most guys with that much money don't get it living by the golden rule. And, like maybe her husband's name—nickname, maybe—is Polo. Maybe Jud befriended this older guy and ended up taking a very successful poke at his wife."

Susan hadn't heard about Polo yet.

"I'll explain in a minute," Dallas said, picking up the phone. He dialed the woman in Bethany. "Going to see how the roses are doing," he said with his hand over the mouthpiece once the line began to ring. "By the way, those damned things cost a fortune. . . ."

Olivia Miles answered on the fourth ring. The ocean and a distant sea gull cry provided background.

"Polo, please," Dallas said.

"I'm sorry . . . ?"

"Is Polo there?"

"I think you have the wrong number."

"Is this . . ." Dallas looked at the circled digits on the phone bill, read them off to her.

"Yes," she answered, hesitated, then, "Who is this?"

"Polo said to call him—"

"No. I think you have the wrong number." She hung up.

Dallas looked at the phone, said to Susan, "There was something weird about that, but I'm damned if I know what it was."

"Good morning." It was well past one o'clock. Dallas greeted T.J.—f.k.a. Teresa Jane—with a smile. He let himself into her room, which was unlocked.

All she had on was one of his shirts, and it wasn't buttoned. "I stole it out of your room. I wanted part of you close to me." Her hair was still tangled and held grains of sand from last night's playing on the beach. She hugged him and the shirt came open.

Dallas caressed her breasts, careful not to scratch her with the letter folded in his hand.

Her lips were soft, kissing him. She pouted when he eased his mouth away.

All these sexy little changes in her were making Dallas have a hard time remembering who she was. "I need you to do something for me."

"Mmm-hmm."

Dallas withdrew one hand—just one—from inside her top. He unfolded the letter with a gentle snap of his wrist and showed it to her.

"Don't hold it so close." T.J. tilted her head back. "I don't have my glasses on."

"It's a letter to a stockbroker."

"F. J. Barnheim's." T.J. read the address. "They're a discount house."

"Which means they buy and trade per a client's order and cut-rate their commission, right? They don't recommend stocks?"

"Basically."

"You recognize any of these?" Dallas poked his thumb beside a list of three stocks, all of which were listed by trade symbol.

"Sure. Endberg Steel, Riviera Bank and Trust, and Gossimer's."

Or EnbrgSt, RvBkTr, and Gossmr, respectively, by trade symbol. All were on the chart Dallas had found in Jud's condo. And here they were again on a letter from Olivia Miles to her discount broker, directing him to sell her out of each *when* — not *if* — they hit a certain price.

"You looking to get in the market?" T.J. snuggled closer. She stroked the back of Dallas's neck, sounding far more lovey than businesslike. "If you are, I'd recommend you stay away from these."

"How come? They've all skyrocketed in the last couple of months."

"They're also being mentioned as part of an insider trader investigation, but you didn't hear that from me. I'd hate to see the SEC come down on you. Federal prison might be a country club, but they still don't offer conjugal visits."

The phone rang.

T.J. said, "Don't answer it."

Dallas kissed her and they hug-walked three steps to the nightstand.

"Don't answer it," she whispered, slipping off the shirt.

Dallas picked up the phone. "No calls."

It was Herbie. "We got big trouble. Big, big, *big* trouble."

Trouble came in all sizes around Ocean City, but big, big, big; triple big; three times big fit only one kind of trouble. Chief Rupert Dawson trouble.

In the Ocean Tides lobby, Dawson was picking through the gratis fruit basket with thick fingers. Sunlight through the window walls highlighted each stalk off the chief's buzz cut like mowed rows of wheat. Herbie was nowhere to be seen.

Dallas said, "All out of beef jerky, Rup."

Dawson considered an apple, then a pear, but instead of eating either, rearranged them like an amateur Rembrandt ready to paint a still life. "You in the mood for a body?'

"What kind of body?"

Dawson changed his mind about the apple. He picked it up, rubbed it down like an umpire working over game balls. "Dead one," he said, crunching half his snack in a single bite.

The four-unit apartment house faced Ocean Highway like a square aqua-blue face with a sagging porch for a smile. Multicolored beach towels hung over the upstairs balconies like limp, wet flags.

As Dawson pulled his cruiser into the tiny parking lot, a college-aged lifeguard wearing OCBP sweats bumped the thick wheels of a Huffy bike down wooden steps from the second floor.

"Over here." Out of the car, Dawson directed Dallas toward a street-level door. His weight raised a creaking moan from the aged porch.

Behind them, on the highway, a group of kids screamed, "Hey, big Huey!" at Dawson from inside a speeding Camaro stripped of its T-tops.

Dawson's size wasn't lost on passersby, especially older kids who thought cops were ludicrous enough, but a fat cop, hell, that was a damned spectacle. Dawson never seemed to hear the mocking, much less acknowledge it.

The huge man struggled to get his fingers inside the handle of a crooked screen door, finally managing the task with his pinkie.

Inside, a sparsely decorated living room with dusty wood floors was dark and depressing with yellowed shades pulled over all the windows.

Dallas heard the girl crying before he saw her. She was curled up on a tattered sofa that had one missing leg supported by a pair of moss-covered bricks. Next to her, a uniformed officer patiently held an open notepad and pen; he didn't seem to be getting anywhere.

Dawson directed Dallas down a narrow hall. "Back here." He worked his apple down to the core and used his front teeth to nibble off remaining strands of fruit.

They stopped at the first of two bedrooms. Cheap pile carpet was peeled up in the doorway; there wasn't any pad beneath it, just dusty floorboard marred with nail holes.

"Hello, Dallas." Sam Paul looked up sorrowfully from beside the body of a young girl. His hound dog eyes hung with the dejection of a Little Leaguer who'd just struck out with the bases loaded. The medical examiner seemed to take death so hard sometimes, Dallas wondered how he stayed in the business.

Then again, Dallas wasn't too keen on corpses either. He tended, as he was doing now, to look the other way. All he'd really noticed about the dead girl was that she was sprawled across the floor like a marionette with her strings slivered.

"Any ideas?" Dawson asked, his voice suddenly accusatory.

"Me?"

Sam Paul went back to the body.

"You been looking for her, haven't you?" Dawson half drilled.

"Uhh . . ." Dallas took a quick glance back toward the body.

Sam Paul was probing her with his eyes at this point, saving the really gruesome stuff until after the body was transported to Salisbury.

The girl was not twenty years old, with oak-brown hair tangled around her face and neck. Her cuffed shorts appeared freshly ironed as did a pale lime T-shirt. She wore white athletic socks, but only one shoe, which was left untied; the Reeboks' twin was tilted on its side like a capsized sailboat near one of the two unmade beds.

"Jeannie Hall," Dawson said, giving the body a name. "We talked to a friend of hers lives near the downtown bridge. She said some guy came around yesterday trying to find Jeannie. And would she call him at the Ocean Tides Motel.

Dallas though, Oh, boy.

"You know, I said it before, now I'll say it again. I'm gettin' a little pissed off your ugly face keeps turnin' up with each dead body." Dawson lifted a window shade and pitched his apple core through an open window. "And I sure's hell would like to know what you know.

Otherwise, a suspicion of murder charge would keep you behind bars till Monday — which is the first time the commissioner'd be available to set bail."

"Don't pull that bullshit with me, Rup. I hate that. There's no such thing as arresting anybody for *suspicion* of anything." Dallas couldn't help his frustration. Five days he'd been working on this case and what? Nothing. It never even looked like a case. Except, lo and behold, dead bodies tended to pop up like lilies after a warm spring shower.

Dallas stuck his hands in his pockets and fought the obscene urge to take another look at the body. "Look, here it is, okay? I'm checking out people who knew Jud Fitch to try and find out why he committed suicide. That's it. Period."

"And she was one of those people?"

"Supposedly." Dallas was beginning to feel claustrophobic in the small apartment. Without air-conditioning, it was as though the heat of the entire summer had been absorbed by the old wood-paneled walls.

Dawson waggled his finger for Dallas to follow him out of the room. In a second bedroom, Dawson closed them inside.

The smell of rotting crab shells made Dallas feel slightly nauseated. Just outside the room's only window, a soggy grocery bag swarming with flies baked beside an overflowing dumpster.

"How much do you know about Judson Fitch? *Really?*" Dawson leaned against a windowsill. "I think you're bein' pretty square with me — square as you ever are — but if you're not, then I'm more than a little pissed. Because this boy is turning out to be involved with some very bad news."

Legally, Dallas didn't have to divulge anything. Teresa Jane was a client and his work for her was legally protected by confidentiality. But Ocean City was, at its heart, a small town. Dallas and Rupert Dawson crossed paths as often as sailboats in a regatta, so practicality meant the rules had to sway with the breezes. Besides, Dawson was hinting that he knew something Dallas didn't, and the only way Dallas was going to find out about it was to trade.

"I've heard about some drug involvement," Dallas confessed, "but nothing concrete. No evidence except one of your boys busting him with a small baggie of grass last week. But . . ." Dallas sighed. He wasn't sure how far to take this. He didn't think he wanted to admit forging Jud's will to get a peak at bank records. "He had come into a pretty big lump of money in a hurry, so it looks like he could have made a run."

Dawson met Dallas's eyes, held them. "Know that body you found under the bed in the Triton's Trumpet?"

Dallas nodded.

"FBI came back with an ID. Jack Rigger. Guy's got a rap sheet. Was a courier for some New York boys — white-collar racketeers who specialize in cleaning dirty money." Dawson readjusted his pose against the windowsill. "The good news, depending on your perspective, is that the thirty-eight we found in Fitch's dresser drawer — the one wrapped in the nightie — didn't kill him. Guy also wasn't killed in the Fitch kid's condo. He got whacked somewheres else — Sam found gravel imbedded in the back of his head, like he fell down on a road somewhere. We're trying to match him with a rented car with Jersey plates we found abandoned a couple miles out of town."

"You're telling me someone kills him outside and then hides him *inside*? Pretty weird isn't it?"

"Yes, it is," Dawson acknowledged.

"I mean you kill someone, you don't bring them home with you."

"Not unless you take them to someone else's condo, because maybe you want to pin the killing on your boy Fitch."

Dallas thought about Jud's stock chart, all the money he'd come into, how he knew to keep bank deposits under $3,500 to avoid routine reporting to the IRS. And now the dead guy in Jud's condo turns out to be a New York money runner.

"Now me, personally," Dawson said. "I don't give a rat's balls what people in New York City do for fun and excitement. They ain't my problem. My job's what goes on within the twelve square miles of this island. Not only 'cause that's what I get paid for, but 'cause it's where I live. I don't cross any bridge out of town I'm not back by sunset. My wife wants to spend the night over Assateague, she takes one of the kids, maybe one of their kids, too, 'long with a big flyswatter for the mosquitoes."

Dawson's wide face was sweating from the heat, dripping onto the girth of his uniform shirt. "Now Fitch's dead. So no way he killed that girl over there." Dawson pointed through the wall. "But I wanna know who did. And I wanna know *yesterday*."

"You know I'd tell you if I knew, Rup. And I don't."

"Okay." Dawson nodded. "Let's try something else. What do you know about Ocean Investments?"

"Fitch's Jaguar was titled in that name."

"You know who else might be involved in Ocean Investments? It's no registered corporation or partnership, I called Assessments and Taxation in Baltimore."

"As far as I know, Fitch was the only one connected to it."

"'Cause we got this call two days ago from someone claiming to be from Ocean Investments. Man's voice, the dispatcher said. Didn't leave his name. He wanted to know if we'd found their company's misplaced green Jaguar. Same car, like you said, the Fitch boy was driving when he got picked up for the marry-wanna. Turns out, the dead girl," Dawson motioned to the adjacent room, "she's been driving the car. She came here with it a few hours ago, according to her friends. Strange thing is, now the car's gone, but the keys to it're still in her handbag."

"So somebody either hot-wired it or had keys of their own. Maybe Ocean Investments gets violent with repossessions."

Dawson shook his head slowly. He pushed away from the wall and headed out of the room.

Dallas followed. Passing the first bedroom, he poked his head in, started to say good-bye to Sam Paul when he saw the three bracelets around the dead girl's forearm. He'd been so busy avoiding the sight of her, he'd missed that before.

"Something wrong?" Sam Paul asked.

Dallas made sure Dawson had continued on into the living room, which he had.

"She was strangled," Sam Paul said, standing.

Dallas crouched and lightly touched the bracelets on the girl's arm. He was cautious with them, as though the act could raise ghosts. They were the same bracelets he'd seen on the girl who'd tried to use Jud Fitch's ATM card the night he died. And this girl had the same length hair, too.

"The killer could have used this," Sam Paul said. "I pulled it off a nail on the ledge. It must've caught when he went out the window." Sam Paul showed Dallas a red bandanna.

"Rup!" Dallas called when he saw it. "Hey, Rup!"

21

"YOU'RE GONNA GET SPOILED," Herbie warned, watching Dallas shave. "Two nice restaurants in one week. That's better than you usually manage for an entire summer."

Showered, with a towel wrapped around his waist, Dallas wiped a clear circle in the fogged mirror. Ventilation at the Ocean Tides was such that even with the door open and an exhaust fan going, a lukewarm shower would cloud the bathroom for a month. "Did Susan tell you?" Dallas asked, straightening his upper lip for the blade.

"About the late Mr. Jack Rigger turning out to be a money runner? Yeah. Pretty sporty, huh? I like white-collar crime."

"You wanna close the door?" Dallas suggested. Herbie stood in the threshold between Dallas's room and the office. "If T.J. would happen to walk in, I don't want her to hear this."

Herbie obliged him. "Doesn't she want to know what you're finding out about her brother?"

"Sure. The other day I asked if she thought Jud might have been selling drugs. She said no, then she said maybe."

"I see." Herbie whistled a few bars of an old Frank Sinatra song. "Then you haven't told her about the body under the bed of Jud's condo, the rich lady girlfriend, or his little list of stocks?"

"That's right." Dallas waved the razor through a gurgling sink of soapy water. The basin continued to drain no matter how hard he tugged the stopper. "No sense in burdening her with speculation." Dallas wiped the mirror again.

124

Herbie nodded. "So the idea is you don't want to say anything to her that might break the mood?"

"You got it."

"How did you manage a reservation in this place?" Dallas asked once they were seated. "They don't take reservations."

"Susan and I rode up here this afternoon. She sweet-talked the manager."

"I bet she did."

Hannah May's was one of the few trendy restaurants in Ocean City where some people actually wore ties. Dallas wasn't among them, but shaved, his hair combed, wearing a button-down shirt and pleated Calvin Klein pants, he fit in right well.

Dallas flapped open the linen napkin folded on his place setting like a swan. He laid it across his lap, then pinged the water goblet with his fingertip. The resulting ring was as crisp and clear as pealing church bells on a cool, fall morning. "Expensive stuff."

Teresa Jane smiled at him. Her hair hung over one bare shoulder in a loose ponytail. "When you were in my room this afternoon . . . when Herbie called and you ran out. . . ." She spoke quietly, her tone fitting the dining room's ambience. "I thought you'd set it up. That you wanted an excuse to get out. I thought maybe you weren't interested anymore."

"Interested in what?"

"In me." T. J. twisted a silver salad fork in her fingers. Her coral-painted nails reflected soft candlelight. "I thought maybe since the suspense was over . . ." She tried to laugh, but managed no more than a smile. "That the *conquest* was over. . . ."

Dallas reached for her hand. "Hey. Don't think like that. That's not true."

Dallas's sincerity was surprisingly, pleasantly, out of character. T.J. met his eyes. "You're sure?" She started to draw her hand away when the busgirl filled their water glasses.

Dallas kept hold of her fingers. "Positive."

It embarrassed her a little, that show of affection in front of a stranger, but Dallas made her suffer through it. An intermediate lesson from the Dallas Henry School of Loosening Up; she'd already passed the introductory phase. Sleeping late, watching lots of bad TV, hell, not cracking a *Wall Street Journal* for days.

"It makes me want to ask how much it would cost to rent my room for the rest of the season. . . ."

In a world of loaded questions, Dallas figured that could have dynamited an entire village. But his silence wasn't hesitation. He was actually basking in the moment. In some very soothing way, he felt as if he had something to offer T.J., and vice versa. Wasn't that how it was supposed to work?

Dallas figured he could get very used to this. And it wasn't the money part, though that did have its seductive power. More so, it was her.

The way she looked sitting across the intimate table. In her "dressy dress," as Dallas referred to it. A strapless bold-print sundress with a slightly V-neck that stopped just short of doing a cleavage plunge. Her slender arms and shoulders, previously masked by starched business suits, now actually blushed with the hint of a tourist's tan.

Suddenly, Dallas wanted the meal to be over with. He wanted the sun, setting bright orange across the bay, to pull the moon up out of the ocean and cast the beach in midnight shadows. He wanted to walk with her through the sea grass, across knolls of virgin dunes, stand before her with the moonglow of the ocean behind her, and watch that sundress slide off her body.

"A dollar," Dallas said after a few moments.

"Pardon?"

"You can have the room for the rest of the summer for a dollar."

"Anything?" Dallas asked.

"I must be bad luck on stakeouts," Herbie complained. "Not a damned thing ever happens."

"Sometimes it's not supposed to." Having excused himself from the dinner table, Dallas was using the pay phone at Hannah May's.

Herbie was posted in his VW, watching Olivia Miles's Bethany Beach house. Figuring the case could withstand a little overhead, Dallas had Herbie pick up a cellular phone from the Rent-All center, which Herbie was now using.

The connection was a little scratchy, as if a bunch of gophers were trying to burrow though the line, but basically the words got through.

"How's dinner?"

"Good."

"Get them to bring an extra basket of croissants and swipe me some, okay?"

"Sure, Herbie. Just keep me posted if anything changes. And if Johnny D shows, call Dawson first."

"You really think he's Polo?"

126

"Who knows. A guy wants to be called Johnny D, maybe his real name's Johnny Polodino."

"I don't buy it."

"You got a better theory?"

"Nope."

"You got the number of this restaurant, right?"

"Sure thing. Kind of makes me feel like the baby-sitter."

$\triangledown$

22

"Mᴍᴍ." T.J. SIGHED. "What did you say?"

"Shh. Don't say anything," Dallas whispered.

"Why?" Naked, smiling, tired, she nuzzled against him.

Her breasts were warm against Dallas's side as he lay across the bed. He propped his head up to watch the ocean.

They were in T.J.'s room, riding out the sustained buzz of Ocean Tides Mai Tais and the climax of what had begun as a long walk on the beach seven hours ago.

Now the drapes were drawn all the way back like theater curtains opened for a stunning world premiere. Outside, beyond the deserted beach, the faint pink glow of sunrise was bashfully spreading along the dark blue horizon.

It was a slow, beautiful, and especially painless invocation as the ocean gave birth to a new day. The infant sun emerged as a halo of glimmering light and built slowly in brightness and strength, dispatching itself into a majestic ascent.

As a band of vital orange spread across the sea, Dallas whispered, "There," and pointed eastward.

Hugging him, T.J.'s gaze followed the direction of his arm as though guided by a navigator's sextant. She saw a school of dolphins gently breaking calm waters with arched gray backs and congenial fins. "My God, they're beautiful. Look at them." She gasped in admiration as they crested the sea.

All around the graceful swimmers, a tranquil, rolling ocean seemed pleased to see her children.

"Listen," Dallas offered quietly. "You can almost hear them singing."

From that distance, it was impossible to hear, but in the silence of dawn, uninterrupted by noisy bulldozers developers had brought to the island, Dallas pretended he could detect each pleasant, fun-shrieked dolphin call as they moved steadily, playfully northward.

He thought if ever given the choice about how he would like to die, that would be it. Swimming with the dolphins, being carried out to sea with them.

Then again, this wasn't so bad either. Dallas sensed his breathing turn steady and restful; he felt that hazy peace that told him he was about half a minute from falling asleep. T.J. covered them both with the sheet and stayed close.

Nice night. Looking lazily around the room as it was brought back to life by the sunrise, Dallas smiled with pleasant fulfillment.

The bedspread was tangled on the floor. Three fluffy pillows were still warm and perfumed from how T.J. had been sprawled across them. Two buttons on the carpet had been torn from her sundress amidst a more rigorous thrust of desire.

From its inception, the evening had been an enjoyable dance, slipping indulgently from a pace that was first slow and tender, then fast and urgent, and back again, and back again . . . and again.

She had, at times, seemed frightened by how readily she accepted him. Yet when they were together, it was so natural, so easy, that even when she'd seemed about to hold back, she had yielded.

No doubt about it, Dallas thought before falling asleep, the beach was a great place to be. That's why he was never leaving. He knew better.

$\triangledown$

23

"**H**E'S DEAD."

"Who?" Dallas stumbled happy sleepy into the Ocean Tides lobby. It was a quarter of two. "Print?"

"Print?" Susan glanced at Herbie, wondering if he knew what Dallas was talking about.

"Yeah." Dallas noticed a ripe cantaloupe sitting on the counter. "Print is dead. No one reads anymore. *Kids* don't read. They can't stand to be away from MTV that long." Dallas picked up the melon, considered its weight. "The gratification in words is not quick enough. Takes too much nurturing. Like this wonderful fruit. Why grow it from seed if you can buy it in a store?" With sleep-tousled hair and bleary eyes, he tossed the melon upward and caught it one-handed. "Where'd this come from anyway?"

"Jason," Susan said.

"Ah, Captain Crunch returns to the sea with his annual melon." Dallas smiled. "It's sort of his offering to the island. Each bite is to be cherished like rare guava."

"Guava is *not* rare," Herbie mumbled.

Susan didn't normally mind Dallas's postcoital spaciness, how he tried to turn everything into a sophomoric poem when he was in love, but, today, work was to be done. She had a stack of legal-sized papers on the counter. Patiently, she said, "Jason said to tell you he's in town for a long weekend. If you want to go sailing he's got his catamaran with him."

"Great!"

"Calvert Miles," Herbie interrupted, ragged from yet another sleepless, fruitless stakeout, "is dead."

"That's a shame. Should we send flowers?" Dallas continued to play catch with Jason's melon.

"It's a little late, boss. He died last year."

"In a boating accident," Susan added.

"Oh . . ." Dallas held the melon. "That's a hint, huh? You don't think I should go sailing with Jas? You know, he's not that bad a sailor. We just call him Captain Crunch for kicks."

"Calvert Miles," Susan said, taking hold of the sheath of papers, "was Olivia Miles's husband. He left an estate that's been inventoried at two million dollars. And it all goes"—Susan flipped four pages deep into her findings and read—" 'to my most dearly beloved wife, Olivia.' "

Slowly, Dallas allowed reality to permeate the veil of ecstasy his night with T.J. had drawn around him like a hedonistic shroud. Olivia Miles. The woman in the Bethany Beach house. The one Jud had called all the time, only to end up with a sorry-but-it's-over letter. Dallas put down the melon. "What kind of boating accident?"

The *Sussex County Flier* reported, September 17, that Calvert Miles, fifty-five, an experienced yachtsman, had piloted his brand-new Whaler boat into the waters of Assawoman Bay on an unusually warm fall day. His vessel was a small outboard, nothing in keeping with the man's financial stature, but he liked little sport boats and it was all he needed because he liked being on the water alone.

There were no witnesses, but apparently the new boat developed engine problems. What the newspaper reported as "unexplained circumstances" caused an explosion that killed Calvert Miles. His body was discovered floating a mile from the wreckage, wearing a bright orange life jacket as brand-spanking-new as the boat.

"Where'd you get all this?" Dallas asked Susan.

"Sussex County Courthouse. And the library."

"Yesterday? When you left early?"

Susan nodded, modest for scoring a coup.

"Sheesh." At his desk, Dallas went further into the papers. There was more. "I thought you went shopping."

Susan rolled her eyes. Sometimes she wondered what decade Dallas had been born into.

"I was going to do this," Dallas said, seeing the deed to the Bethany

Beach house, what had been Susan's starting point. "I was . . . really." He looked for a substituted deed, the one by which the estate would have transferred the property from Calvert Miles and Olivia Miles solely to Olivia Miles, but it wasn't there.

"The estate's still open," Susan said, knowing what he was looking for.

"Then how'd you know he was dead just from checking title?"

"I had a hunch."

Dallas cringed. His ego was taking a severe beating this morning — this afternoon. How had she come up with that? It ran contrary to how they'd been thinking; that the reason Jud had made short calls to the Bethany Beach house was because when Olivia's husband answered, he hung up. But the husband was cold in the ground by the time those calls had taken place.

"You think she had her husband killed?" Dallas felt conspicuous asking the question, like maybe there was some obvious point he'd missed.

Susan went even deeper into the papers she'd copied at the courthouse. "Olivia and Calvert Miles were married fifteen years ago." Susan pointed to an uncertified copy of their Sussex County marriage certificate. "He was forty, previously unmarried. She was twenty-two. Also previously unmarried. The wedding made the society pages." Susan had copied the article and underlined key phrases. " 'Calvert Miles, noted Delaware industrialist with an estimated net worth of fifteen million dollars . . .' "

"Fifteen million? But his estate's only worth two million."

"He's waking up," Herbie noted.

"There's this." Susan turned the page.

In Re Calvert T. Miles, Petition To Establish Guardianship
of the Person and Property.

"What's this about?" The ten-page court document had been filed one year prior to Calvert's death.

"Olivia got herself a Dover lawyer and two Wilmington doctors who went before the court to establish Calvert's incompetency."

Dallas flipped ahead to the judge's order marked DENIED. "It didn't work."

"As well it shouldn't have. According to the petition, three months before Olivia filed for the guardianship, Calvert suffered a slight stroke,

132

but he recovered fully. He wasn't mentally or physically incapacitated. The doctors admitted that. The argument was that Calvert was no longer able to comprehend sophisticated and intricate business dealings, as had been his forte. Yet he was still investing in them. Right before his stroke, Calvert was swindled on a Caribbean land scheme. Solely on the basis of a very slickly printed prospectus, he went in as a major limited partner in a new hotel in Barbados. The pictures were nice — there's a copy attached to the petition — but the financial data was so inconsistent a second-year finance major could have seen what was wrong. That the deal was a fraud. But Calvert Miles bought in and lost five million dollars."

Dallas groaned.

"And apparently it wasn't the first time he'd been conned. But instead of being more careful the next time around, Calvert became desperate. He wanted each new deal to make up for his past losses. And the hole kept getting deeper and deeper. His net worth was down to half a million when this petition was filed."

"No wonder his wife tried to have him found incompetent." Dallas scanned the petition. "But he must have done something right to get his estate back up to two mil."

"I can't document any of that. But there's also this." Susan turned past the guardianship papers. "A lawsuit filed by Olivia against the company that underwrote Calvert's life insurance. They refused to pay because of the circumstances surrounding his death."

"You mean they thought Olivia killed him? That would be their only basis to withhold benefits."

"There were rumors Olivia was having an affair. That Calvert's health, his age, his failed business dealings, and loss of wealth were all motives for Olivia to want him dead. The case was settled when the insurance company couldn't implicate her, but they did turn up an interesting tidbit. One night, a young man was seen going into Olivia's beach house with his own key."

"Her suspected *love-aire*," Herbie chimed in with a French accent.

Susan continued. "Whoever he was, he spotted the insurance investigator staking the place out. And threatened to kill him."

Dallas remembered what Jens had said about Jud picking a fight with her boyfriend.

"And Monsieur Casanova's description . . . ?" Herbie offered.

Dallas supplied the answer. "Looks a lot like Jud."

"Bingo-ringo."

Dallas considered his informed associates. "You guys think Jud and Olivia offed the husband?"

Herbie shrugged. "Nice job if they did."

"Sweet timing," Susan added.

"Then again, boss," Herbie reasoned, "boats do blow up. Defects with a new motor. Courts're full of products liability cases."

Dallas held out one hand, measured off an inch and a half. "I'm this far from a visit to Momma Rosa. See if her crystal ball knows what happened to Jud Fitch."

"Well," Susan said, tugging three stapled pages from beneath his elbow, "there's *also* this."

"My brain capacity is threatening overload."

The switchboard rang in the lobby with an incoming call. Herbie headed out to answer it.

Susan pressed the papers in front of Dallas. "Jud's assets are a little better than the forty grand he's got in Second Coastal S and L." She showed Dallas the deed to the party house.

Dallas read the grantee clause. "Ocean Investments."

"Took title June ten. Paid five hundred grand cash. And look who signed for the company." On the last page, Susan poked her finger to the notarized signature. "Judson Fitch."

Herbie returned from the lobby. "That was Chief Dawson on the phone. Johnny D has an airtight alibi for the strangled girl yesterday. Cops've cut him loose."

Dallas dropped his head on the desk like a rock.

The girl with pale freckles was washing her long red hair. Bent over the kitchen sink, her shorts rode high up pink-tanned legs. Her baggy white tank top got splashed as she rinsed out suds beneath a goose-necked faucet.

"Hello?" Dallas rapped against the screen door and it rattled against warped molding.

The girl didn't hear him for the water. No one else seemed to be home. On the floor, seam-weary sofa cushions were arranged in a makeshift bed. On top of a dusty old TV, rabbit ear antennas were positioned like a referee's signals gone haywire.

"Hello?" Dallas called again when the girl turned off the water.

She draped her head with a thin towel and slowly made her way to the front door. She was the one who'd stayed inside the first time Dallas had come calling. "Jeannie is dead," she said flatly. Her voice and eyes seemed distant. Her top was wet and stuck opaquely to her breasts, revealing small pale nipples through white fabric.

"I'm sorry."

"Maybe I should have told you what you wanted to know. We didn't know who you were." Lazily toweling her hair, she turned back into the center of the room. "You can come in. But it's not much cooler inside." She walked past an open carton of milk left standing on a foldaway table. Her motions were slow, almost indolent. She sat in a mod sixties-style chair, a round cushion centered on a cylindrical base. Bent forward, her kinky hair hung nearly to the floor. What'd you say your name was?"

"Dallas."

"Right," she said from inside the towel, "like Texas."

"You never told me yours."

"Linda." Beside her feet were two rolled joints and a tin ashtray littered with crisp roaches.

"Linda, do you know who might have killed Jeannie?" Dallas played it carefully. He wasn't sure why she'd been suspicious of him the other day, but not now.

"I guess the same person who killed Jud."

"What makes you think he was killed?"

"Jeannie was there when it happened." She began to dry her long hair, making it look like the beginning of a tired, protracted ritual.

In an earthy way, Dallas found her attractive. She wouldn't be the type of girl to date surfers or weight lifters. Her own lack of pretension seemed to indicate she wouldn't find that sort of narcissism attractive in any guy.

"Jeannie said when she first saw the blur in the darkness — something falling — she thought it was a big bag or something. It happened so fast, it took her a while to realize there had been arms and legs."

"Wait a minute. How did it happen? How was Jud killed?"

Linda dropped the towel into her lap. "I don't know exactly. Jeannie never got that real straight because she didn't actually see who did it. She was waiting in the car while Jud went up to see *the man*." She made that sound sarcastic.

"The man?"

"Whoever Jud was working with."

"Working with doing what?"

Her eyes roamed the room with dreamy imprecision. "I don't know."

135

Dallas sat in an orange chair. His arm rested on the card table between two economy-size boxes of generic corn flakes. The thick smell of sour milk oozing from an open container churned in his nostrils.

"What exactly did Jeannie see?"

"She saw him fall."

"But did she see if someone pushed him or if he did it on his own?"

"You can think what you want." Linda seemed convinced he'd been killed. "Like I said, Jeannie was waiting for Jud in the car. When she saw the body I guess she went into shock. She didn't hang around to ask questions. She came back here. I thought she was stoned, really tripping out she was so gone. She could barely talk and was shaking all over. She didn't even know how she'd gotten here even though she had the keys to Jud's car."

"Why didn't she go to the police?"

"She was afraid." Linda barely moved as she spoke; slouched in the circular seat, she didn't bother brushing away a fly that crawled along her shoulder. "The day after, once she realized she had Jud's car, she figured whoever killed Jud would know that someone had been there with him—whoever had the car would know he'd been killed. Jeannie knew they'd look for the car and look for her. So she booked. She went home to try to get it together, then figured she'd come back to drop off the car somewhere. That if she did that, and never told the cops anything, whoever killed Jud would leave her alone." Linda stared straight ahead. "I thought it made sense. But I guess not."

"Do you know why Jeannie would have tried to get money out of Jud's bank account? From a money machine?"

"I know he gave her a card. To impress her." Linda's words rolled easily off her tongue in a stream of uninhibited thought. "Jeannie never had much money, she was always scraping to get by. Her folks either. They'd come down here in a falling-apart old station wagon, I think it embarrassed Jeannie. They were great people, and she loved them, but she couldn't get over the fact that her dad wasn't some big corporate muckity-muck or something. Because she hung with that kind of crowd. The kids' fathers were always loaded. Like Jud's. So when he told her to use the bank card whenever she wanted, it about blew her mind. Jud knew he was buying her, but it didn't matter. He didn't love her, didn't care what happened to her, but she never saw that all he wanted was to get between her legs." Linda looked around. Homing in on the rolled joints, she picked one up. "You have a lighter? Matches?"

When Dallas shook his head she started on a semi-zombieish hunt for a source of flame. "You know, Jeannie was a virgin before this summer — one of those wait-till-I'm-married girls — which's fine, but Jud sure blew away her morality with a little green. She'd have done anything for him. Anywhere. Anytime. And that really seemed to pump Jud up — that he'd bought himself a slave. He loved that *power*. He was addicted to it. It was his disease."

Linda turned on the gas stove, held her hair back as she leaned close to the burner and deeply breathed the spliff to life. "But that's every man's dream, isn't it?" As she smoked the joint, Linda took intense pleasure in each deep toke. "Money, power, a slave girl or two, or three."

The sweet smell of burning ganja tempted Dallas to join in, lose everything that was wrong with the world in the convenient swirl of a pacifying haze.

Oftentimes, most of the time, it didn't matter that the problems would still be there when the easy rush was over. That the drugs wouldn't solve anything wasn't reason not to indulge. The concept was one of escape. Because the world would always be too big, the problems never ending, so what difference did it make if one more unpleasantry was left unresolved?

Dallas said, "If you thought Jeannie was in trouble, why didn't *you* call the police?"

Linda smiled ironically; she held a deep lung of intoxicating smoke, then exhaled. "My other roommate's boyfriend pushes crack to ten-year-olds. My little brother steals radar detectors and busts hood ornaments off Mercedeses and BMWs and sells them. The girl in the apartment next door steals a hundred bucks a night from the bar where she works; she doesn't get caught because the manager's skimming so much he can't trace it." Linda held the moist end of the joint to her pale lips. "So who would you have me tell the police about first, Dallas?"

$$\triangledown$$

24

"OH, MAN, WHEEW, YOU scared me. I thought you were one of
the owners." Waist deep in the shallow end, the pool boy breathed a
sigh of relief. Relaxed after his momentary fright, Adam fell backward
into clear water.

A girl was in the party house pool with him. She held on to the edge,
keeping her back coyly to Dallas since she was topless. It was almost
better than if she'd been facing him head on. Dallas found bare backs
arousing, but he was an easy mark that way.

"I'm not supposed to mess around," Adam said, swimming an easy
sidestroke, "but it's kind of like *Ferris Bueller's Day Off*, you know. Ever
seen that on tape? Where he says sometimes you just gotta stop and
experience life, otherwise it passes you by?"

Dallas's tennis shirt stuck to his back with perspiration. The ride up
in the 280 had been unusually hot, as if the air just wouldn't breathe a
sigh of relief today. Even the marsh grass, with its feet in bay waters,
seemed wilted by the heat.

Dallas envied Adam, coasting through summer days pretending he
was cleaning pools just to stay out of the weather. Maybe if the people
who owned the party house were around more often, their pool
wouldn't get such thorough attention.

"Do you know where they are?" Dallas asked. "The Wisemans?"
He'd made note of their name the other day when Adam told him. It
would be nice to know their relationship to Judson and Ocean Investments, the owners of record of the house they lived in.

"Haven't seen 'em for a while now. Lisa either, I'm sorry to say."
Adam willingly said that in the presence of his topless girlfriend.

"Are they New Yorkers?"

"I don't know. I don't think so."

"Have you ever seen whether their car has New York, maybe New Jersey plates?"

"Mmm, nah."

Of course, Dallas figured, why would Adam notice things like that? The important things, when the Wisemans would be out of town, how hot their daughter was, that's what he'd know.

"You think it would be okay if I went inside and looked around?" Dallas glanced toward the open sun room door, where the girl's bikini top lay beside the hot tub. "It's a pretty neat house and I'm a big architecture nut." He knew that sounded lame, but it was too hot to think up a really good lie.

"Oh, man. I don't know." With a bright sky above, Adam squinted at Dallas. "I mean, I'm sure it would be okay, but, like, you know, I don't know who you are." He seemed uncomfortable having said that — acting maybe too suspicious — so he quickly added, "I'm sure it's okay. But I can't risk it. Swimming in their pool's one thing, but if for some reason they didn't want — "

Dallas held up his hand. "It's okay. Don't worry about it." He smiled at the girl, who averted her eyes. "I'll come back some other time." Dallas waved as though it was the last physical effort he'd be able to manage until the heat broke.

He retreated around the side of the house and looked for a way to break in. His best bet was a tall window on the rear side. At night, going in that way, he'd be able to steal between the beams of floodlights aimed over the lawn more as decoration than security. He'd also be secluded from the view of neighboring homes thanks to how the party house backed to the bay. What bothered him the most was the outdoor motion detector Adam said guarded the pool. That could make things dicey.

Then again, by tonight, someone might be home, which would spike the idea completely. The prospect of being mistaken for a prowler — which, technically, legally, he would be — didn't thrill Dallas. Getting shot at was low on his list of pleasures, right around being arrested. Unfortunately, he'd had experience with both.

About to get back into the hot-box 280, Dallas heard the topless girl's happy squeal carry over the house. The two kids romped in the water. "No, Adam, *no!*" she shrieked, as if she was trying halfheartedly to keep him from tugging off her bottoms.

Dallas wondered how come he was the only one who seemed to be working today? Dallas hated that.

Sometimes the only thing to do was binge. Dallas stopped at the Food Lion and loaded up. Store-made lemon meringue pie. Breyers butter pecan ice cream. Soft Batch chocolate fudge cookies. Dip-size Fritos. Barbecue Ruffles. A pint of sour cream and a packet of Hidden Valley ranch dressing. Two pounds of ground beef. Sharp cheddar cheese. A crispy head of lettuce. Hot Old El Paso salsa and pickled jalapeños. Three Vidalia onions and a bunch of scallions. Taco shells. Dole pineapple/orange juice and Rose's grenadine.

He made sure the checkout lady gave him paper bags, not the jellyfish plastic ones, and carried his purchases triumphantly back to the 280. Through it all, he had a hard time keeping his smile from making him look like a lunatic.

Driving down Coastal Highway, he swerved into the bus lane, ran red lights, beeped at cute girls crossing the road after a full day on the beach, and played *Led Zeppelin IV* so loud on the tape deck he could barely hear himself think.

At the Ocean Tides, he put a closed sign over the office door and called in the troops — Susan, Herbie, T.J., Chad, and Chad's girlfriend with the green bikini.

Susan tended a lavish tropical bar.

Herbie cooked up masterful tacos and spoke nothing but Spanish, to which Dallas, seemingly inseparable from T.J., replied, "*No comprendo.*"

In Dallas's room, they made too much noise, ate too much, drank too much, and churned up a mess that would probably have Edith and Missouri — the Ocean Tides's maids — demanding a raise before they'd even consider cleaning it up.

A few times, Chad tried to explain to his girlfriend that Dallas was not his father, but for some reason or another, the girl couldn't hear him. Usually, it was due to Dallas singing a very off-key rendition of his own tune, the one he'd been working on for years and was going to send to Jimmy Buffett when it was perfect:

Mai Tais and tacos,
guacamole dip and burritos,

if you are what you eat,
I'd be down under six feet,
    dancing with the worms and the grubs.

Yet it was in that wonderfully loose and aroused state that Dallas had a vision. Not so much a premonition as it was a resorting and resifting of the past week's events. Things didn't make much more sense, but they were now confused in a particular order.

About to topple arm in arm with a giddy T.J. onto the bed, Dallas grabbed Herbie's bony arm for support.

"*Que pasa*, boss?"

"Mi amigo, I'm gonna pass out now. But wake me in five hours." Dallas attempted to tap his temple, but nearly poked his eye out. "Esta noche, resolvamos problemas."

Loosely translated from butchered Spanish: Tonight, we find answers.

$\triangledown$

25

"Can you hear me?"

"Is that you or Kate Smith?"

"Come on, Herbie, don't screw around. Can you hear me or not?"

"How about a few rousing choruses of 'God Bless America.' "

"Go to hell." Under a humid blanket of darkness, Dallas was up to his chin in swamp grass.

Where feathery blades of vegetation had gone to seed they teased his face like a fan dancer's boa. Even wearing a long-sleeved T-shirt and jeans, he felt as if hordes of crawly bugs had arisen from the murky lowlands to eat him alive; he could sense their ticklish antennae searching his flesh for a vulnerable spot to strike with pincer teeth.

Having entered the mucky extreme of the bay seventy yards south, Dallas had carefully maneuvered his way through the night, his eyes making good use of a flat moon. He tested spongy earth to make sure nothing more than his ankles plunked into a seaside stew ripe with rotting crab carcasses and gurgling frogs. Now, holding the earphone in place, he was within sight of the party house.

Herbie had concocted the communications rigs two years ago with various component parts grabbed off the shelf at Radio Shack. He and Dallas were each equipped with earplug receivers and quarter-size throat microphones powered by a battery pack/component board; the whole package fit into their hip pockets as snugly as a wallet filled with hundred-dollar bills. Connecting the transceiver to the battery pack was a black wire the width and texture of overcooked linguine.

Primitive-looking as it was, the gizmo allowed the two of them to keep in secretive communication within a half mile range. It functioned equally well on stakeouts or breaking and enterings — the only thing the equipment was selective about was fresh batteries.

Herbie sang a few bars of "I Want to Be in Pictures" from his post on the side street, where his feet were dry in the VW Bug.

Dallas swatted a mosquito that buzzed his forehead, lured by the sweet scent of his perspiration. He wished his transmitter could send electric shocks — just little ones, enough to get Herbie's attention. "Call the house again," Dallas said once Herbie stopped doing his Kate Smith, or was it Ethel Merman?

"Nobody's home, trust me. The windows are dark. Not a creature is stirring, not even a murderer."

"Humor me . . . since I'm the one going in."

"No sweat."

Dallas could hear Herbie hitting the pushbuttons of the portable phone, each touch of his finger resulting in a bell-tone beep. "Make sure it's the right number."

"Boss, I been calling for the last hour. I can even hear it ring inside the house from here."

Dallas took out his earplug and listened over the belch of crickets fanning across bay shallows. The sound was distant and muffled, but distinctly a ringing one, coming through the glass walls of the sun room. Dallas tried to remember if he'd seen a phone in there. "Yeah, okay," he told Herbie, sticking his earphone back in, "I hear it, too."

"Okey-chobee trail."

Dallas started forward, pulling his back foot from slurpy marsh with a quiet pop of burst suction. Like swimming the breaststroke on land, he reached his hands forward into furry sea grass and spread it aside.

Each step was gingerly considered, knowing a sinkhole could swallow him waist deep in slimy gunk. Following a course parallel to the edge of the bulkhead, he began to feel slightly panicked with claustrophobia, as though being consumed by the tall vines. He kept glancing up to a silver sky of warm haze and faint stars to beat the psychological threat.

It was the longest way to the vulnerable side of the party house — where he'd spotted a window of entry that afternoon — but Herbie assured him that by remaining undercover of the thick grass and bulkhead, the outdoor motion detector would be blocked from picking him up.

"You there yet?" Herbie's question squelched into his ear.

"About twenty yards to go. Everything still clear your side?"

"Yupsee doodle." Herbie sang the chorus of "No Business Like Show Business" when he stopped his words on a dime. "Whoops. Spoke too soon. I got two — no, three — people north of the house . . . crossing the street. . . ."

Dallas stopped. "I thought you said nothing happened when you went on stakeouts?"

"You must be bad luck." Herbie's banter lost some of its nonchalance. "Okay, what are they up to here?" he asked out loud.

"What do they look like?"

"They're in the dark . . . wait a minute . . . lemme see. Okay, no big deal, three kids, all male, about fifteen, with swimming trunks and towels. Running across the street into the backyard. You see them now?"

Dallas parted the grass and looked toward the rear of the party house. He saw three kids dash through a path of bright floodlights at the corner. They were heading for the pool, bare feet padding across green lawn, hitting the concrete patio without losing speed, then diving feet first into the shallow end.

Three consecutive splashes broke the night's silence and quieted nearby frogs. One of the boys surfaced with a loud, "Woooh!"

"Quiet, Todd," another one hissed.

"Ah, Christ, I think I broke my foot," the third kid said with a laugh. "I thought this was the deep end."

"Will you two be quiet before the cops come!"

"We're not eighteen. They can't arrest us."

Dallas said, "Hey, Herbie . . ."

"Yeah, boss, I'm thinking the same thing."

"The pool boy forgot to turn the goddamned motion detector back on."

Herbie said, "Hell, we could've used a sofa."

The kids' covert pool hop only lasted five minutes before they were scared out of the water by a nearby car door.

"What was that?" Dallas asked, scratching and itching in the sea grass.

"Neighbor," Herbie reported from around front. "Older man with a grocery bag going inside the house two down. No problem."

Towels around their necks, the three boys paused at the corner of the house, then broke into a run across the side street.

"All right," Dallas decided, "the hell with this mess." He crawled out of the marsh and vaulted the bulkhead. His shoes were sticky with brown muck as were his jeans from the ankles down. Sitting on a darkened section of warm grass, he peeled off the shoes, socks, and pants, then continued up to the house barefoot, down to the gym shorts he had on beneath the jeans. "Here goes," he announced, slightly winded. "Keep an eye and ear out."

"Then I'll only have one of each."

Wrapping his muddy-legged jeans around his fist, Dallas punched hard against a small pane of glass in the sun room door. Framed between squares of decorative molding, the glass shattered with a firm pop, then danced across the brick floor like tiny fireworks.

"Okay?" he asked Herbie, reaching in to unlock the door.

"You do it?"

"Yeah. I'm in."

"Nice job. Didn't hear a thing."

"Amazing what you can learn from your clients." Dallas circled the hot tub, feeling its humidity. The odor of chlorine burned his nostrils with a chemical smart. In pale moonlight, he saw the portable phone lying against the brick floor. "Dark in here," he reported through the throat mike. He moved stealthily into the living room, careful not to knock into anything.

Central air-conditioning hummed quietly, laying a refreshing chill over the interior. Dallas sniffed a lingering antiseptic odor, like the cleaning crew had been resolved not to leave a trace of the party they'd tidied up days before.

"This is weird," Dallas said, able to make out vague details by incidental light showing through opened curtains. "There's no books here. No magazines. No cigarettes. No CD's or tapes." He snooped around the high-tech entertainment center that seemed dwarfed beside the big-screen Mitsubishi. "It's more like a furniture store than a house. Plenty of places to sit, but nothing to do."

Dallas moved on to the spacious, terra-cotta-tiled kitchen. Scandinavian cabinets and the refrigerator were void of anything edible. "I feel like I'm in the twilight zone. The other night this place was overflowing with chips and dip. Now there's not even half a jar of mustard."

"Maybe Ocean Investments is on a diet," Herbie commented from the car.

"I think they've moved out." Dallas shut the refrigerator door, blacking out the light its interior had washed across the room. He played with the drink dispenser mounted to the side-by-side door; squirting cold jets of water over his finger, he wiped his forehead with the cool relief. "We still okay out front?"

"Yup."

"I'm going upstairs.

"It is not so much an obsession with money, as a lust for it. There is a pulse to money, and it feeds our hunger for the pleasures that are only attainable from its bounty.

"Now it is true," the recorded voice argued with itself, "that money cannot buy health, that health is wealth that only a sick man can see, but is there really any denying that money can buy longevity? That without personal resources, hospitals allow sick people to die who could otherwise be saved. Those who have the resources are allowed to live a few years longer, during which time there will be countless visits — *paying* visits — back to the hospital, to help feed the doctors' own particular lusts for pleasures. Pleasures that only money — lots of money — can buy."

Dallas listened to the tape player and found himself somewhat hypnotized by it. The speaker was at once captivating and frightening, for in the logic of his argument was a scintilla of madness.

Dallas was up on the third floor of the party house, in the crow's-nest attic that had a 360-degree view through spotless glass windows of the entire island.

In the distance, the bright lights of Maryland's slender coastline sparkled in the warm dark haze like flecks of gold. Lighted buoys bobbed atop a rising tide on the bay.

The six-walled room was unlike any other portion of the party house. Here, a comfortable obedience to chic decor yielded to the cluttered studies of a secret student. Crooked store-bought shelves had been strung haphazardly beneath each window. Dog-eared paperbacks and spine-weary hardcovers were packed so tightly together they seemed to hold the shelves in place, as though pulling out the wrong book would topple the stacks of printed words like tentative dominoes.

The only lighting was provided by a trio of slender reading lamps secured to plaster walls by carelessly tooled screws. Close to each lamp was a slant-backed canvas chair, and beside each chair was a stack of books awaiting consumption like a line of oysters before a shucker's knife.

Economics. Philosophy. Theology. Psychology. Terrorism. Those were the topics of choice, the basis around which the library had been built. The only anomalies were glitzy biographies on dead rock stars: Janis Joplin, Jimi Hendrix, Jim Morrison, John Lennon. Dallas flipped through one of the less heady titles he recognized, a popular, mass market self-help book on "winning." Nearly every page had been viciously marked in red pen. Certain passages were denounced either simply as "bullshit," or, more pretentiously, as "hackneyed meaninglessness." Another segment had been editorialized with bold letters scratched so hard as to nearly tear through the page. *"This is how to succeed?"* the critic's words demanded. *"Only in dreams. Babies' dreams."*

The tape continued to play as Dallas knelt on the floor and scanned other titles, opening certain volumes to find that each had been similarly marked by red pen, with the captioned phrases either denounced or praised.

"There is no service in the world anymore," the voice proclaimed. "Nothing is done out of charity. It is essential to remember that. That people make that claim is only proof of how deeply they have concealed their own claims for money. How they hide their greed behind masks of worthiness. Nothing, nothing is done for a communal good. Everything is self-motivated, self-induced, for self-pleasure. A person's interest in another's happiness is only to the extent that it will enhance his own success.

"What does this mean to me? This is how every event in human existence is to be interpreted. And any occurrence that takes place can be used for profit, it can be analyzed and made into money if the opportunity is seized by the right individual. And why should that quest for money be limited to following a certain path? There is no guarantee that life holds security for anyone. People work lifetimes for companies with the hope — with the assumption — that the pension plan they contribute to for their entire working life will provide for their golden years. But when the company goes bankrupt, the pension plan washes out, and what happens to the man who spent his entire life frugally setting the money aside so that his final years could be consumed by expense-covered trips to a series of doctors whose only desire is to keep the man alive so that he can get sick again and come back?"

Dallas opened a manila file folder. The top page was a stock chart, just like the one he'd found in Jud's condo. Although this one dated back further than Jud's by almost two years. The list included those same companies again, the ones from Jud's chart and Olivia Miles's letter to her discount broker. EnbrgSt, RvBkTr, and Gossmr.

Further into the folder was a list of bank accounts, over a dozen, each assigned a different name and Social Security number. The weird thing was, attached to each person's account was a photocopy of his birth and death certificates. Each of them had been born approximately twenty years ago, but none had lived more than five years. What the hell . . . ?

On the tape, the speaker sighed in admiration. "God, it is such a perfect business, medicine. Use just enough technology to keep people alive, but don't make them well. It's a gold mine, a virtual goddamned gold mine."

As the speaker's voice grew even more potent, Dallas tried to recall where he'd heard it before. The quality of the tape was poor, but in the enunciation, the voice pattern, there was something familiar. He started to fast forward through a long pause, but then the lecture continued:

"So if doctors can keep people alive, suffering just enough to need them . . . and lawyers can create complex laws that are impossible to interpret just to assure themselves a lifetime of work . . . and chemical companies can market sugar substitutes they know cause cancer . . . and automobile makers put vehicles on the road that are unsafe . . . is there really any limit, any conscience to making money? Or is the business ethic just a fraud to allow a shallow conscience a full night's sleep? A way for corporations to claim the *law* says their first duty is to make money for their stockholders, and that the means of making that money can be as subversive as undermining a foreign government or murdering to keep secret scientific breakthroughs that would render the company's products obsolete?"

The words seemed to smile now as their speaker drew aim on his own theory. "There is nothing that money cannot buy, cannot answer, cannot do. Therefore, there is nothing, positively nothing that *cannot* be done to make money. *It is all legitimate.* It is all moral. It is all obtainable. All one needs is the stomach to realize what is true, and the nerve to go through with it."

Dallas stared at a wall of books as loud static played out to the end of the tape. Maybe he didn't recognize the voice. Maybe it was because its preaching tone sounded like Teresa Jane that Dallas had the sense that he had just been listening to a tape of her brother, Jud.

One way to find out. He took the cassette from the portable recorder and slipped it into his shorts pocket. Then he replaced his transceiver earplug in time to hear Herbie shouting:

"Boss! Boss! For chrissake, get out! Two guys coming into the house. Two guys!"

Dallas bolted for the stairs, hustled down to the second floor and was about to vault the staircase to the ground floor when the front door opened and in walked Johnny D and Adam the pool boy.

Now Dallas knew whose voice was on the tape.

26

"THIS'LL ONLY TAKE a second."

"Yeah, whatever," Johnny D said to Adam.

Now what the hell was the pool boy doing with Johnny D? They seemed as likely a twosome as calm seas in a hurricane.

Dallas listened to them move through the spacious first floor.

When their footsteps moved toward the back of the house, Dallas eased a few steps down from the second-floor landing. To get out the front door, he'd have to follow the stairs as they turned toward the rear of the house, then make an about-face in the foyer.

At least he was barefoot; the chance of making noise was lessened. All he'd have to worry about was someone turning a corner and seeing him — no trivial concern.

He was on the landing, aimed away from view of the front door when Herbie's whisper threaded cautiously into his earplug.

"Tap the mike once if you're okay?" Herbie was as tense as a slaughterhouse turkey.

Dallas gave the throat mike a single, firm jab.

Herbie sighed relief. "If you want me to call the cops, tap twice."

Dallas answered with a distinct, single beat.

"Okay . . . I'll hang tight till I hear from you," Herbie advised, then quieted.

Dallas eased down onto the next step, wincing when the stair tread creaked under his weight.

"Goddamnit!" the pool boy swore, stepping angrily back into the

150

house. "Goddamn kids busted out the back window to get into the hot tub. Little bastards. There's still wet footprints out on the patio." He went into the kitchen and banged around in one of the closets, grabbing something, but Dallas couldn't see what. "I'm sorry we didn't catch them. I'd have liked to bust their trespassing little asses."

Johnny D didn't reply.

Adam said, "Make sure everything's okay upstairs. And be quick about it. I've gotta be in New York by dawn.

Dallas hustled back up to the second floor when Johnny D started his slow ascent up the carpeted stairs. As though he could sense the pursuit of Johnny D's breath on his neck, Dallas ducked into a second-floor bathroom. There, dim light was allowed in through a small window that faced the street.

Peering outside, Dallas saw Herbie's VW and could almost sense his faithful partner squirming in the tiny car.

When Johnny D turned on the hall light, Dallas felt as if he'd been nailed. He eased into the bathtub and gently slid the flamingo curtain closed to conceal himself.

Johnny D went through both bedrooms.

Downstairs, Adam was on the phone. "Mickey? Yeah, Adam Walker, how yah doing? Listen, I'm in a bit of a jam. Can you get the Cessna ready for me? Gas her up, put her on the runway. I'll be there in . . . fifteen minutes." Adam paused a beat, then, "Thanks. You're a winner."

Adam hung up the phone as Johnny D walked past the bathroom door. Johnny D cast an aggressive shadow as his search continued lackadaisically into the small loft area. But he turned the light to that room off as quickly as he'd snapped it on, then killed the hall light and withdrew to the first floor without bothering to check the crow's nest. Like this was wasting his time.

His hiding place once again veiled in darkness, Dallas leaned back against the tiled shower wall and listened to muffled conversation downstairs. The house was fairly open, but different ceiling heights seemed to play with the words as the sounds carried up to him.

"Goddamn kids," Adam said again, dumping shards of glass into the kitchen trash can.

"It's okay," Johnny D reported. "I checked everywhere."

"All right. Good." Adam sounded relieved. "Hold this a second for me, would you?"

"Yeah."

The gunshot boomed through the house like a cannot blast.

Dallas jerked reflexively as he heard Herbie screaming "No!" through the earplug.

"Herbie!" Dallas whispered harshly. "Herbie!" Stepping out of the bath stall, he looked through the street-front window and saw his friend hurrying from the VW, running toward the front door.

Herbie's long, scraggly hair thrashed frantically across his shoulders. "Herbie! Go back, damnit! *Herbie!*"

Downstairs, an efficient squeak of heels crossed the foyer, going for the front door.

"Herbie!" Dallas lost sight of him beneath overhanging roof lines.

The front door latch was unbolted. Someone exited the house. Then the door closed. Adam, the pool boy, emerged from beneath the small front porch. Calmly, he got into the 4-Runner parked in the drive, turned over the engine, and pulled off.

"Herbie?" Dallas whispered into the mike. He hurried from the bathroom, not sure what he was going to find downstairs, but convinced it wouldn't be pretty.

The party house was dark again, all the lights off.

"Herbie, you okay?"

"I've been impaled by a goddamned holly bush. What the hell happened in there?"

"Get back in the car. Call for an ambulance."

"You okay?"

"Yeah, but I think Johnny D may have ridden the wave of no return."

In the foyer, Dallas started looking around, ready to avert his glance because he wasn't a big fan of blood. But his adrenaline was pumping so high, when he found it, he stared in shocked disbelief.

Johnny D was sprawled lifelessly over the floor, wearing his trio of trademark bandannas. There really wasn't much left to the side of Johnny D's head. What had seconds earlier been a cohesive wad of skull and brains looked to have been churned up by an aggressive food processor, then regurgitated over the kitchen wall and floor.

Adam had not only used a high-powered handgun, but had done so poking its barrel within inches of Johnny D's temple. And he'd been quick and efficient about it, too, not giving the surfer time to react.

Dallas ran out to the car, his bare feet not conscious of tiny stones digging into his soles. "Let's catch him." He knocked over Herbie's Big Gulp resting on the floorboards, splashing chunks of ice and sticky soft drink in a cool slush around his ankles. "He's going to the airport."

Herbie had holly leaves tangled in his wild hair from jumping into the bushes to avoid Adam at the front door. He looked a bit of the deranged Roman emperor as he whined the VW engine to life, then · lurched them forward into first gear.

"How do you work this thing?" Dallas demanded, picking up the portable phone.

Rather than explain it, Herbie steered with one hand and used the other for dialing. "Cops?" he presumed.

"As many as we can get."

Traffic was tight going toward the inlet. Pushing the VW to its minimal limits, Herbie weaved through tourists who were determined not to interrupt the slow pace of their vacation for any emergency — especially some long-haired leftover freak from the sixties, which was what Herbie looked like as he barely avoided the bumper of a station wagon with Quebec tags.

"Damned Nordiques!" Herbie shouted.

Dallas had his feet braced against the Bug's age-worn dashboard.

By the time they reached Twenty-eighth Street, there was still no sign of Adam Walker's 4-Runner.

But when a duo of light-flashing police cars sped up from behind in the bus lane, Dallas was encouraged. "We'll make up time now. Pull in behind them."

Herbie did as instructed, then had to slam on the brakes when a van cut off both cop cars and Herbie in order to get the last parking space in the Jolly Roger lot.

"Asshole!" Herbie screamed.

Behind the van's wheel was a bearded pipe smoker from Pennsylvania — the worst possible demographics for a driver in the mid-Atlantic region.

Convinced a crash was imminent, Dallas put his arms over his head.

Herbie swung the Bug into a 360-degree turn that shot them through an onslaught of protesting horns without a scratch.

Dallas checked his limbs in disbelief. All of him was still there.

"We were doing better without the cops," Herbie complained, speeding down the center lane.

By the time they reached the Division Street Bridge, the VW had a fifty-yard advantage on a pack of screaming police cars.

Dallas was on the portable phone, giving Rupert Dawson a description of Adam the pool boy.

"He killed the other suspect we arrested?" Even through the scratchy connection, Dawson was incredulous.

"Yes."

"You're sure!"

"I was in the goddamned house."

"Why don't you ever call *before* all hell breaks loose?"

"What've I got, a crystal ball?"

On the bridge, without a maze of sightseeing tourists to hold them back, the urgent police convoy overtook Herbie's VW in a blitz of speed that nearly sucked a row of bait-weary fishermen off the draw span's sidewalk.

By the time they reached Route 611 and turned left, there were eight cop cars in all — what Dallas figured to be the entire night shift. They rolled down dual-lane highway through a cut of aged pine trees.

The lightless road burst alive with danger as its usual serenity was overtaken by bright headlights and wailing sirens.

The procession dead-ended fiercely at the small two-story structure that acted as the tiny airport's control tower and terminal. Sirens were cut off. Wary flashers continued to throw off bright streaks of light that failed to synchronize with control tower beams.

Just beyond a chain fence dotted with no trespassing signs was half a mile of runway marked with blue and white lights.

Now that they were here, none of the cops seemed to know what to do, only that they were going to do it with shotguns. Busting out of their cruisers, they seemed to be looking for someone with a *Shoot me!* flag on his back.

Herbie's VW was blocked from the runway by cop cars. Dallas sprinted for the control tower stairs.

"Where is he!" Chief Dawson shouted after Dallas, looking around as his cohorts broke out flashlights.

Check the hanger. Don't let anybody out! Block off the parking lot!" Dallas grabbed the door handle and rushed into the meager control room.

"What the hell's goin' on?" A country fly-boy traffic controller was looking over the runway, where cops were covering the single hanger and going through the empty terminal.

"Where's Adam Walker?"

"Out there." The controller pointed a long finger toward the end of the runway, where flashing wing lights flared rapidly in the darkness.

The vague silhouette of a twin-engine prop plane turned profile to the tower, then faced head on as the loud whirl of accelerated engines accumulated power.

"Who's in the plane with him?"

"Nobody."

Dallas turned out of the tower, hit the aluminum stairwell with both hands on the railings and slid to ground level. "Don't let him take off!" He ran to the concrete runway that sliced through the same forest of pines that lined Route 611. "Down there, Rup! Down there!" Waving his arms, Dallas got the big chief's attention.

The twin-engine plane gathered speed — coming at him.

"Block the goddamned runway, Rup!"

The plane was quickly parallel with stalled police cars, its wheels skimming the ground as its turned-up flaps began to nose the red-and-white striped craft upward.

Dallas dove from its ascent path, hurdling runway lights as he rolled over in dewy grass. "Stop the goddamned plane, Rup! Shoot it down! Shoot it down!"

In the roar of the plane's engine and the rush of confusion — cops only half sure why they were on the scene — Dallas's plea to the chief was misinterpreted by some as an order.

Most of the force were seasonal gendarmes who worked civilian jobs in the wintertime as teachers or shoe salesmen, and all spring, going through training on the range, they'd fantasized about letting go with a few rounds.

The trouble was, they were as poor as marksmen as they were eager to display the fact. The night erupted in flashes of bright orange and white light as bullets and shotgun pellets flew everywhere.

A runway light less than ten feet from Dallas's head exploded with a direct hit. Tree limbs were scratched as their trunks charitably prevented potentially fatal rounds from carrying into neighboring trailer parks.

Chief Dawson stood seemingly impenetrable in the middle of the melee, ordering his troops to cease-fire.

And Dallas watched Adam the pool boy's twin-engine Cessna pull higher and higher into the distant night.

The plane drew a steep ascent toward the stars in the eastern sky, its wing lights flashing like blistering supernovas light years away, growing ever smaller on the wide-open horizon.

As the final errant blast of gunfire was silenced by Dawson's demand, and the acrid scent of gunpowder floated through humid air like the ruinous scent of a fatal flower, Adam Walker passed over Ocean City's barrier coastline. He made his escape toward the Atlantic, banking north.

Two hours later, in the police station, Dallas was still working on a statement about how Johnny D had been killed by Adam. Going over details with the town's lone homicide detective who'd been called out of bed to deal with this.

Chief Dawson stuck his head in as Dallas was wrapping things up. "We got your boy."

"What?"

Dawson sounded unusually happy considering the evening's events. "We must've hit the plane."

"What're you talking about?"

"We got a call about an hour and a half ago from the dredging barge. They reported an explosion half a mile out around Tenth Street. Coast Guard got there in a hurry and found the wreckage of your boy's plane. He went down."

"Jesus." Dallas sat upright.

"Divers'll start looking for the body tomorrow."

$\bigtriangledown$

27

THE STANDING LAMP BESIDE the sofa in T.J.'s room cast her in pale golden light. It was just bright enough to attract a pair of dragon-flies who slow-danced lightly against the screen.

Above all else, T.J. hadn't wanted him to talk about her brother. Hadn't expected it. But when he did, she no longer felt comfortable with her robe left unbelted; the fact that she wore nothing beneath in order to attract Dallas into another lost night of simple, sensual plea-sures rifled her with guilt.

Dallas didn't really want to talk about it either. It had been too nice, the way they'd slipped from their concern with her brother's ill-fated death into a fantasy of summer lovers. The switch had been as obliging and smooth as the outgoing tide beneath a purple sunset, but, now, Dallas sensed that the return of reality would be at least as traumatic as he'd feared. Because it always was.

Slowly, he began to outline all that he had kept from her: Jud's sudden wealth; his involvement with Olivia Miles and a mystery man named Polo; his link to the party house where a seemingly naïve pool boy had turned cold-blooded killer and then gone down in a plane crash; that Jud had had a stock chart with issues rumored to be linked to insider trading, and that records of those same stocks had turned up in the party house and in a letter from Olivia Miles to her stockbroker; how the girl who had been with Jud the night he died was now also dead; how a murdered courier had been found in Jud's Triton's

Trumpet condo (a place he bragged about to his friends and then later denied renting); the unexplained visit of Jud's father.

Once Dallas gave all that he knew to T.J., she sat somberly on the sofa and stared straight ahead. Not looking at Dallas but beyond him, as though lingering in the air were visions of the past where his words were taking shape and she could actually see the events he had just described.

What finally broke her stare were tears. And for the first time since her brother's death, Teresa Jane Fitch cried—doing so not only because Judson had died but because of what had died in her.

When Dallas tried to comfort her, she resisted his hug and his sobriety deepened. For the past few days, a fantasy—the beach—had allowed her to become someone she really wasn't, someone she had, in some ways, wanted to be. But now, brutal actuality was dragging her back to the life in which she had so long been trapped, and would, most likely, soon become consumed again.

In the darkness of his room, Dallas played the cassette he'd taken from the party house crow's nest. In light of recent events, he heard the maniacal voice much more clearly. It wasn't Jud, it was Adam Walker, the pool boy.

Dallas recalled the first day he'd met Adam, how Adam talked about removing obstacles that would keep him from being successful, or something like that. It had seemed perfectly sophomoric at the time, until Dallas considered such a philosophy along with what he was listening to on the tape.

Hell, Adam was no innocent, wide-eyed college senior cleaning pools to pass the summer. His ambition had spawned a mutant American Dream turned insane with greed. He'd become a calculating killer who saw fit to get rid of anything in his way—like Johnny D and Jeannie.

Jeannie Hall had been strangled with a red bandanna. Dallas had missed that at first: Adam's motive to kill her. It wasn't until he saw Johnny D's body in the party house wearing all three bandannas that he recalled the first day he'd seen Adam at the pool. Adam, vacuuming an already spotless pool, had wiped his face with a large, red handkerchief. A red bandanna was the only real piece of evidence left behind at the scene of Jeannie's murder. As though whoever had done the killings was purposefully leaving an obvious clue in hopes of pinning the crime on someone else—just as the courier's body had been left in Jud's condo.

Something else Dallas realized about that afternoon at the pool: Adam had graciously volunteered to examine the list of names Dallas had been given by Terry. There were all Jud's friends for Adam's examination. Included on it was Jeannie Hall, the potential witness who'd driven away in Ocean Investments' Jaguar the night Jud had died, driven away in the car the killer — and Dallas was now convinced there had been a killer — wouldn't have been able to find if he'd searched the parking lot after the murder.

The reason Adam would have been worried about that was that he was Jud's killer. It fit.

Adam occupied the party house crow's nest, so Dallas figured he also owned it. Everyone Dallas had talked to said Polo owned the party house, except Adam, who said it belonged to people named Wiseman. One possible explanation was that Adam was the only one who knew truth from summer rumor; but what Dallas believed was that Adam had reason to lie about Polo, because Adam was not only a killer, he was also Polo.

But why had he killed Jud? What had their relationship been? Had Adam simply been Jud's source for the drugs he'd been selling? And how did the courier fit in? Were the drugs coming down from New York? And what was Ocean Investments all about? And Olivia Miles, she was a real problem. Seemingly Jud's ex-lover, she traded stocks about which Jud and Adam also kept records.

Dallas thought, the stocks. The stocks. What was it about those damned stocks?

It was after four in the morning when Dallas got out of bed.

In the Ocean Tides lobby, Herbie sleepily contemplated the *Evening Sun* crossword puzzle.

Dallas moved into the office doorway, wearing a wrinkled T-shirt and dark blue Jockey underwear. "He's alive."

"What?"

"Adam Walker is still alive. No way in hell one of these cops hit that plane. He faked the explosion."

"Come on." Herbie rested the folded-over paper on his knee. "Walker couldn't have known ahead of time that we'd end up chasing him, that cops would be chasing him. That anybody'd *shoot* at him. There wasn't time to set it up."

"But there was." Printed across the chest of Dallas's T-shirt was a bold, red iron-on: YOU'VE SEEN OUR BEACH . . . NOW *GO HOME!*

"While I'm nosing around the party house, talking to him, Adam starts feeding me this lie about people named Wiseman owning the place. And I agree with him. So Adam looks at me and knows he's a liar talking to a liar. He probably doesn't know what I'm up to, but it's enough to get him thinking his scam might be in trouble. Where he got lucky was with the timing of his getaway tonight. That was better than he could have ever hoped. You see, he was covering his ass all around, because he was going to disappear. And if he doesn't want anyone looking for him, what better way to prevent that than being dead." Dallas shrugged. "Plane blows up. He *must* be dead, right?"

Herbie was all too pleased to set aside the crossword, which had suddenly, by comparison to the braids of Jud Fitch's case, become an all too unexciting pastime.

"And something else," Dallas said. "Olivia Miles? The woman in the beach house in Bethany? Her husband died when his boat engine exploded."

Herbie smiled. "Son of a bitch."

The police cars—two from Bethany Beach, one from Ocean City— were already at Olivia Miles's when Dallas and Herbie arrived. There was also an ambulance.

"What the hell?" Dallas wondered. He parked at the cul-de-sac of Sea Knoll Court. He and Herbie proceeded up the lantern-lit driveway and were about to try the door when Chief Dawson loomed into view from a dark penumbra of shrubs beside the house.

Hatless, as always, the chief was cast in overhead light that shadowed his bull skull and made it seem as though he didn't have any neck at all.

"Little out of your jurisdiction, aren't you, Rup?"

The big man's hand moved down across his forehead and eyes, ending with a pinching wipe of sweating nose. He looked at something that stuck to the end of a stubby finger, then flicked it into the bushes. "I'm beginning to wonder what kind of witness you'd make."

"How's that?"

"Adam Walker?"

"Yeah?"

"He's who you said was flying that plane that blew up?"

"That's what the air controller told me."

"Uh-huh. Well, we got an Adam Walker—matches the description of the kid you gave me—inside here." Dawson rapped his knuckles against the siding.

Dallas triumphantly backhanded Herbie's skinny bicep. "I told you he was still alive."

Dawson shook his head. "I said he was in there. Didn't say anything about him being alive." The chief reached for the polished brass doorknob. "Woman in there shot him dead when he tried breaking in."

Olivia Miles stared numbly at a ceramic objet d'art on the glass coffee table. She sat back against the soft cushions of a long plush sofa with her hands folded in the lap of an ice-green robe. From beneath the cotton garment's shin-length hem appeared the lacy edge of a very expensive piece of lingerie, something the uniformed officer taking her statement would have liked to see more of.

Frankly, the cop was a whole hell of a lot more interested in Olivia's clothing than in detailing a report from an obviously shocked woman who had just killed a prowler.

Fashioned in pale rose tones with gray highlights, the living room covered the entire ocean front of the house. Two seating areas were established by an arrangement of pricey condo sofas and soft tub chairs made of splashy island-motif prints. One section was oriented toward a beach view through a floor-to-ceiling window, while the other was for more intimate tête-à-têtes, when the attraction was the company.

Dallas first saw Olivia Miles from the foyer, picking up her reflection in a mirrored wall that made the living room seem even more expansive.

Olivia caught sight of the newcomers and tried not to let it register that Dallas was familiar. She didn't seem sure from where she knew him, but his presence had at least a subtle effect on her composure.

"Would you mind if I got another glass of water?" Olivia spoke in a weak voice to the young man in the uniform. Before he could approve, she proceeded to the kitchen, her gait unsteady, as if she hadn't eaten in days. She clutched the counter, using the time to compose herself and get another look at Dallas.

When their eyes met, Dallas felt her suspicion penetrating him. Casually, he turned his back and went down on one knee, acting as though he'd found something interesting buried in the thick pile carpet.

"Did you find his car?" Dallas asked just loud enough for Rupert Dawson and Herbie to hear.

Bethany Beach was an entire state line out of Dawson's jurisdiction, so he was keeping out of the way, letting a yuppie-ish detective with short-trimmed hair and a Brooks Brothers' knockoff suit confer with the Sussex County coroner.

"Now how would I know what he was drivin'?" Dawson asked conspiratorially.

"Try a green Jaguar."

"Fitch boy's car."

Dallas nodded.

"Who are these men?" the Bethany Beach detective demanded of Dawson from across the room, pointing to Dallas and Herbie.

Having lodged her protest, a concerned Olivia Miles stood beside the nappy cop with a refilled glass of cold water.

Off her left shoulder, the uniformed officer who'd been taking her statement leaned back to get a better look at the ankle-length nightie peaking from beneath her robe.

"They're not reporters," the suit said, his voice adding the inference that they better not be.

"They're with me," was all Rupert Dawson answered before lumbering out the front door.

Dallas wondered if any of the four cops in the room — the suit and his three uniformed helpers — or even the coroner noticed that Olivia Miles didn't seem at all bothered standing so close to Adam Walker's body.

And it was Adam Walker. Lying dead in a puddle of blood sure to test the carpet's Stainmaster guarantee. He was on his side, his feet not a yard from the sliding glass door he had used to gain entrance. His clothes were damp and stiff as though just drying from a swim in the ocean.

The door was closed. There was a single hole in it, where the bullet that had gone precisely through Adam's chest — taking lots of necessary pulmonary functions with it — and continued out into the night. Presumably that slug was now lying bloody on the beach, where it would either wash out with the tide for the next millennium or be discovered by some high-tech bum (as C.J. called retirees manning metal detectors).

The uniformed officer with the crush on Olivia's nightie offered to take her back to the sofa. He placed a gentle hand on her elbow and she accepted.

When she bumped into the coffee table, her surprise was bona fide, because she hadn't been watching where she was going. Her attention — and her memory — remained focused on Dallas, wondering what he was looking for as he stepped around the coroner and examined the glass door.

It was unlocked. As he opened it, warm night air seeped into the

162

cool living room, passing over Adam Walker's body like a specter. "He came in this way?" Dallas asked the yuppie cop.

"Yes." The head cop's name was Alexander Hampton—"Like South Hampton," he'd always say, as though his surname was especially tricky. He was more than a little miffed with Dallas's presence, but since his chief and Rupert Dawson were old school friends, he knew not to cross Ocean City's taskmaster. If it had been up to him, he wouldn't even have called Dawson, but he knew there was no way he could deny suspecting this Adam Walker was the same person the Ocean City cops had sent out a description of earlier that night.

"No sign of forced entry," Dallas pointed out.

The cop stood, smiled with false sincerity as he brushed the neat lapel of his suit jacket. "No shit. She forgot to lock it."

"That the gun?" Dallas gestured to a .44 Colt Python sealed in a clear plastic evidence bag beside the coroner's black valise.

Hampton paused, as though answering questions took years off his life expectancy. "Yes."

"Registered?"

"She thinks so, but she's not sure. *I* plan to check that out . . . if it makes you feel better."

"Yeah, those unregistered guns are usually so much more dangerous than the registered ones."

Hampton figured that was a sideswipe at him, but wasn't sure. "She bought it after her husband's death. Because she was frightened living alone."

"Uh-huh." Dallas looked around. She was frightened living alone but left her doors unlocked—come on Hampton, wake up. "Did your body there have a weapon?"

"No. The house was dark. He obviously assumed no one was home."

Jeez, Dallas thought, old Hampton had swallowed Olivia's version of events like a shark in a feeding frenzy.

But the fact that Olivia Miles had a majority of allies didn't seem completely comforting to her. Acting visibly upset on the sofa, she seemed intent on gaining unanimous approval. Clutching the front of her robe, she trembled with tested nerves.

Her cop friend sensed her distress and asked if she'd like to leave the room. She declined.

"Hey, doc." Dallas tapped the coroner's shoulder.

The older, white-haired gentleman continued poking around Adam Walker's ears. "What?" He sounded tired and bored.

"How come his clothes are wet?"

"Now how would I know? I'm a physician, not a fashion consultant." The doctor preferred nights when he could sleep through. Like back when he was in private practice, before his malpractice carrier and HMOs had driven him into public service. He cursed insurance companies and prayed that God would strike them all as dead as the bodies he was summoned to autopsy at all hours of the day and night.

Dallas wished Sam Paul were handling Adam's body. He'd have liked to get Sam's reading on the corpse's vibes. Dallas bet if his spirit talked, Adam Walker would say, "Color me surprised." Or, maybe, "Color me screwed."

"I guess," Dallas said after a few moments, keeping his eye on Olivia in the mirror, "she just got lucky and nailed him with a good shot, huh?"

"That's a fine hypothesis." Hampton nodded, then, having withstood all he could from a T-shirted intruder, demanded, "Do you have a purpose here?"

Dallas turned to face Olivia Miles head on. Making sure they were eye to eye. "Not really. I just deliver flowers."

$\triangledown$

28

"Another flower?"

Dallas shook his head. "Nah. I stole this one earlier on the way out." Dallas twisted the blood red rose by its thorny stem. Its blossom was as full and lush as moist lips on a wanton summer night.

"Come in." Olivia Miles retreated into the foyer. Her auburn hair flowed over the shoulders of a slinky beige blouse. On her body, even beach-worn jeans looked expensive. "I must admit, you have me puzzled."

Passing through the foyer, Dallas dropped the rose back into its vase. "Likewise." Dallas followed her into the living room.

Adam Walker's body had been removed, but his blood left behind an amorphous souvenir dried into the tight weave of mauve carpeting. Beyond Adam's semifinal resting place, through the decorative bay window, the sun rose like a cookie cutter circle in a silk blue sky.

She sat on the orchid-patterned sofa facing the big window. Crossing her legs, she leaned forward, resting an elbow on her slender knee. The front of her blouse fell open with practiced allure.

Dallas imagined her as a beautiful jellyfish. A man-of-war with swaying, delicate tendrils of splendid purples, blues, and reds — moving with sensual, yet deadly deliberation, able to kill with the same potency with which she attracted.

Dallas unfolded the *Dear Judson* note from his hip pocket and handed it to her. "You want to explain this?"

Olivia smiled sadly at the words she had written less than two weeks before. "He was a sweet boy. If only things hadn't been so . . . confusing."

Turning toward the sunrise, she closed her eyes and leaned back. "Are you with the police?" All of her feigned nervousness and shock had departed along with her audience.

"No."

"So you don't have a tape recorder with you?"

"Want me to undress so you can see for yourself?"

She opened her eyes, seemingly stirred by his proposition. "Some other time." As though it truly was a possibility.

"Jud Fitch's family hired me to find out why he committed suicide. *If* he committed suicide."

Olivia shook her head. "Not his family. It must be his sister. Judson didn't care for anyone else in the family. Nor they for him. Teresa Jane, I think her name was."

Dallas didn't comment.

"He loved her deeply, you know. But he felt betrayed by her. Growing up, it had always been the two of them against their father. They made a pact that when they were old enough, they'd break away from him and start new lives. But when Teresa Jane followed her father's demands and went into business, Judson knew his father had won again. It was like she was on his side now."

Even knowing Olivia's involvement, Dallas couldn't help the way he felt looking at her. Her beauty went a long way to disguise deadly motives. "I know you murdered him."

"Who?" She seemed genuinely surprised by the accusation.

Dallas pointed to the bloodstain. "Adam Walker."

"Oh, for a moment I thought you meant Judson. It's obvious I killed Adam."

"I said murdered. As in malice aforethought."

"The man was breaking into my home."

"I don't think so."

"How can you say that?"

"I found a letter in your mailbox you addressed to your stockbroker. It concerned a number of companies that have been linked to insider trading. Jud had a near-identical list of stocks, so did Adam. I think the three of you had some chummy arrangement. I also know your husband died in an explosion, that you were suspected but cleared, and now it looks as though Adam Walker tried to fake his death the same way."

"Are you here to blackmail me?" She leaned back and rested her arm across the sofa cushions. In the process, the front of her blouse strained open at a rather nice angle, as though she would offer her body

166

as an opening bid if this was going to become a serious negotiation.

"I'm not looking for money if that's what you mean."

"How un-American."

"And I don't really care about how anyone rips off the stock market. I figure the odds are better in Vegas anyway. I also don't care much that Adam Walker is dead. What I want to know about is what happened to Jud Fitch and why. You tell me and maybe I go away and keep quiet. If you give me some crap about not knowing what I'm talking about or you'll have to call your lawyer, then I'm going to grab every cop, SEC agent, and newspaper reporter I can find and tell them what I know. Granted, it might all be entirely circumstantial, but it would certainly arouse their interest."

Olivia thought for a moment. "I didn't kill Judson."

"Which means someone else did?"

"I thought you knew that already. Maybe you don't know much at all. Maybe I'm better off *not* telling you."

"Your decision." When she didn't reply either way, Dallas pressed on. "How the hell did you meet Jud? And Adam Walker? How does something like this even get started?"

"That's the magical thing about the beach — I'm sorry, I don't know your name."

"Dallas."

"That's a sweet name." She said "sweet" lustfully as though seduction were only half a beat away. "The wonderful thing about the beach, Dallas, is that everyone comes here. You meet the most remarkable people. And the most remarkable things happen." She seemed awed by the possibilities. "You may want to sit down, this will take a few moments." Her body language invited Dallas to sit beside her, but Dallas wasn't biting — because he figured *she* did, like a cobra.

He sat on the floor with his legs outstretched. Bits of sand escaped the footprint of his Nikes and disappeared into the carpet. He leaned against the sliding glass door. "Who killed Jud?"

"Passion." Olivia looked at Dallas, playing a sort of sexy hide-and-seek with her eyes.

"No riddles. Who killed him? A name."

"Adam." She sighed his name fondly.

"You mean Polo?"

Olivia nodded. "I gave him that nickname. Don't you like it?"

"And Adam — *Polo* — killed Jud?"

"Maybe it's easier if I tell it from the beginning. It started when my

167

husband was still alive. Calvert was a sweet man, but he was older, beginning to fail. He understood that he couldn't fulfill my sexual needs."

"And God forbid you forgo them."

The affront didn't even graze her. "Calvert also understood opportunity. That life was fleeting. And certain pleasures can only be experienced at certain times, certain ages. Like a train that passes through a particular station once per century. If you miss it," Olivia shrugged, "you miss it forever."

"Adam was your lover?"

"Yes."

"Did your husband know about him?"

"Calvert knew I had lovers, but he didn't know who they were. He didn't want to know. Of course, he didn't want other people to know either."

"So you had to be discreet?"

"Yes."

Dallas wasn't sure he was going for this; she sounded convincing enough, sincere enough, but the most successful con artists always did.

"I was seeing Adam when Calvert suffered his stroke."

"No cause and effect there, I suppose?"

Olivia smiled. "I am long beyond guilt, Dallas. That was something else Calvert taught me."

Another teacher maimed by his student, Dallas thought.

"When Calvert got sick, while he was recovering, I had to take care of our finances. Which I had never been privy to before except for signing joint tax returns. I knew when we were married Calvert was reportedly worth fifteen to twenty million. So when I found Calvert's net worth was *under* a million right after his stroke, you can imagine my surprise."

"And fear," Dallas added, but held up his hand. "Sorry. I forgot you're past all that guilt stuff."

"You are a smartass, aren't you?" The accusation was benign. "I like that. Jud was a smartass." She stood. "Would you like something to drink, Dallas?"

"Sure. A little arsenic on the rocks."

"Coming right up."

"And a rat poison chaser."

Olivia headed toward the kitchen. "Sorry, I'm out. Liquid Drano all right?"

Dallas laughed — nervously. God, but she was cold. Less than twelve hours ago she'd shot her lover stone dead; his bloodstains were still in the carpet and she was making jokes.

Olivia plunked ice cubes into rocks glasses. Dallas watched her on the other side of the breakfast counter. "I found out Calvert had lost a lot of money investing in terrible businesses. Some were outright frauds. Shortly before his stroke, he put five million into a limited partnership that was building a hotel in the Caribbean. It turned out to be a scam."

In spite of what she said, Dallas guessed Olivia did have a conscience. That was twice now she'd linked her husband's stroke to the loss of money.

"The fact that he was failing — *had* been failing — humiliated my husband." Olivia splashed gin into two glasses and tossed some soda on top of that. "Once he lost money on a project, Calvert became obsessed to make up that loss and then some. And to do it in a hurry. Which made him an even easier mark for the next bad deal."

"How does Adam fit in?"

"When I told him about Calvert losing so much money, Adam became very concerned." Olivia handed Dallas a glass. "And it's not what you think."

"I'm not thinking anything," Dallas lied. "I'm just listening."

"No." Olivia sipped her drink, stood by the door. "You're thinking that Adam had hopes of marrying me once Calvert was dead and that he'd be rich as a result."

"Was I thinking that?"

"But Adam, at that time, was already well on his way to being richer than Calvert. *On his own.*"

"You're going to tell me Adam made money buying and selling stocks. And I'm going to say, fine, where'd he get his seed money? You can't make money *without* money. And I'm going to look at you and say you're where he got his stake — that you stole it from your husband, then had to cover it up so he didn't find out. When a competency hearing didn't work, you had to kill him."

"Adam," Olivia explained, her tone of voice making it clear Dallas's theory was wrong, "was a very intense young man, very ambitious. When he was only a freshman in college, he managed to get interviews with dozens of New York banks and brokerage houses and, obviously, his zealousness showed. He had that fire people look for."

She drank a little more gin. "As chance would have it, Adam met a stockbroker who had a wealth of inside information. And nothing he could do with it. Insider trading is illegal. But what if there was a way to pass along this information to someone outside of his brokerage house, some unrelated third party? Someone who would buy and sell the stocks for the broker instead of the other way around?"

Dallas didn't follow her right away.

"They started slowly, Adam and the broker. The broker sent Adam money — always in cash and by courier — and Adam invested it how the broker told him to, usually through discount brokers. Then, whenever Adam sold a stock — when the broker *told* him to sell it — the courier came back for the cash, of which Adam was allowed to keep ten, fifteen, as much as twenty-five percent of the profits for his end of the deal.

"Slowly, over time, the broker's faith in Adam deepened. Adam discovered how easy it was to open bank accounts under false names. He tracked down birth certificates of people who had died, people who would have been about his age had they lived, and obtained social security numbers for them which he needed to open bank and broker-age accounts. That way, Adam could spread out the buy of a single stock over dozens of identities, which further camouflaged what was really happening.

"The broker started sending more and more money. The deals got bigger. And Adam was no dummy. He invested his own money — what he'd been making off the broker — in these same stocks. Every penny he could get, he put into these deals. Adam was getting incredibly rich, but his life-style remained unchanged on the surface. He knew flashing money was a sure way to raise suspicion. So whatever he bought, he bought in someone else's name or a company name, anything to cover it up."

Dallas saw the light. "And Adam let you in on it."

"When I told him about Calvert losing so much money, Adam said there was a way he could make it back for me." Olivia shook her head. "But Calvert wouldn't allow it. Adam even talked to him directly. The two of them sat in this very room." Olivia looked down at her feet.

She seemed troubled, by what Dallas wasn't sure, but he guessed she spent so much time trying to deny true feelings that sometimes all that emotion got confused, like waking up from a dream unsure about what's real and what's not.

"I think he knew," Olivia said slowly. "I think Calvert sensed Adam and I were having an affair. I think that's why he said no to buying Adam's stocks." She turned her head. "He didn't speak to me for days.

170

All along he'd said it was all right for me to see other men, I'm sure he *knew* in his heart that I *was* seeing other men, but actually to meet one of them face to face, that must have been . . . must have been very . . . difficult for him."

Emasculating, Dallas was going to say, but didn't.

Olivia took a cleansing breath. "Adam suggested I file for a guardianship. He'd talked to a lawyer who said it could be done, so I went along. It was a terrible thing to do. Airing Calvert's misery like that in court, letting everyone see what a failure he'd become after a life of success. . . ." Her voice trailed away. "But what else was there? What could I do?"

"You killed him," Dallas accused, and Olivia's head shot up.

Her eyes burned for his. "No." Denying it forcefully, then, softer: "No." She looked at the ugly spot on her rug as though it were Adam. "*He* killed him. Adam killed him. Two weeks before it happened, Adam said he had a present coming for me. A surprise. He wouldn't say what. We talked about it every day. Adam was very playful, he liked teasing me that way. Then Calvert was killed in the explosion and Adam stopped talking about the present. He went back to college right after it happened. And I knew what he'd done."

"But you didn't tell the police."

Olivia drew a breath. "I had an alibi. I was out of town with my aunt. They found the timing very suspicious but couldn't prove anything." Olivia straightened her back. "I didn't know Adam was going to do it. And if I'd told the police about it . . . ? They would have implicated me as a part of the plan. So I just let it lie."

"Until last night?"

Olivia stepped on the bloodstain and said righteously, "Until last night."

Adam's had been a simple plan of escape. Over the past two years, he'd accumulated so many identities, so much money, all of it without paying taxes, it was like digging a deep hole and then oiling the walls. There was no way out. Eventually the IRS, the SEC, all those good federal agencies with frightening initials would catch up. They were slow but steady like that.

There was also the ROTC. Dallas had nearly forgotten Adam telling him about his service commitment after college, and, certainly, the armed forces weren't any place for a millionaire.

Adam feared that his New York stockbroker, the one feeding him the inside information, the one who'd started the whole scam, might eventually get burned. Which could take Adam down with him. So, in a very bold move, Adam had made his usual rendezvous with the courier, handed off the cash—which Olivia said was as much as half a million at a shot—and then murdered the courier, stashed the body under Jud's bed, and stolen the money.

Jud, on the other hand, was more than just a loose end. Olivia explained that, too. Originally, Adam brought Jud in on the stock deals because he wanted to prove something to him. It had started three months before Jud's death.

Like a lot of kids after money, both boys were intensely competitive and jealous. Adam resented Jud's banking pedigree, that all Jud had to do was waltz through college and he'd be in at a bank, a brokerage house, wherever he wanted to be. So Adam was going to show Jud a thing or two about the stock market.

Jud got a taste for making illicit money fast, and it spread through him like cancer. Like Adam, it also made him a little crazy. Everything lost its proper perspective.

Adam kept reminding Jud who it was who'd shown him the ropes, to whom Jud *owed* his good fortune. But Jud was used to being on top, he liked—*needed*—people to be looking up to him. So Jud found a way to get back at Adam. He seduced Adam's girlfriend; he went to bed with Olivia, got Olivia to fall in love with him. She was afraid of Adam by that time, anyway, so it was easy.

Adam found out and went crazy. He told Olivia if she didn't stop seeing Jud he'd kill them both. Olivia wrote Jud a note—the one Dallas found—saying it was over. She either hung up on him or cut him short when he tried phoning her.

Jud knew he'd gotten under Adam's skin, he just didn't know how far. And Jud rubbed it in. That night at the Atlantis, Adam had arranged to meet Jud. They argued and Adam killed him, probably with Johnny D's help, Olivia said. Adam had taken on Johnny D as a henchman, thinking all tough rich guys had bodyguards and yes-men.

After Jud's death, Adam told Olivia she was going to have to go along with his plan or he'd kill her, too. Adam's idea was to take out his plane, ditch it in the ocean, and blow the plane up. No one—not the IRS, SEC, ROTC, not even Adam's broker—would come looking for a dead man. He would assume one of his false identities, consolidate all his money in a foreign bank account, and Olivia would be with him. Damned decent plan for a college kid.

Only Olivia knew she couldn't be with him anymore. She told Adam to come to the house after he faked the plane crash; to come in the side door with his key—just like the night he'd threatened the insurance investigator looking into her husband's death. And as soon as he came through the door, Olivia shot him. He was bleeding, gasping for breath, when she picked his house key off the floor and stuck it in her pocket.

"In spite of everything," Olivia said, defending herself, "I did love my husband. And Adam knew that."

Slowly, Dallas pulled himself to his feet. His hands were stuffed deep in the pockets of his jeans, pants that were as worn as Olivia's, but not nearly as alluring—so maybe he needed a better top than a wrinkled T-shirt.

He looked at the bullet hole in the glass door, fractured threads spreading from it like the fingers of a frozen anemone. The sun was rising farther above the horizon, leaving the brilliant colors of daybreak behind.

Dallas was still worried—for Teresa Jane's sake—about one detail. He dreaded the answer as he asked: "Adam's crooked stockbroker . . . ? Was it Jud's father?"

Olivia held his eyes fondly for a few seconds before answering. "No, it wasn't Jud's father."

Dallas nodded, accepting her reply.

There was hurt in her eyes, perhaps recalling sadly how what had begun with such simple intentions of pleasure had turned dangerous so quickly. "Is that all you want to know?"

Dallas knew she was really asking what he was going to do, who he was going to tell. "I think," Dallas said, "unless someone at the SEC gets exceptionally meticulous, you're going to get away with it."

"I hope so," she said.

Dallas gave her half a nod. "It's hell being rich, isn't it?"

Olivia escorted him to the front door, handing him a rose from the Waterford vase. "The most magical things happen at the beach, Dallas. Always remember that."

"I find it hard not to." He strolled down the curving driveway between lanterns still lit from the dark night. At the curb, Dallas turned over his shoulder and waved good-bye with the rose.

Looking glorious, glamorous, she disappeared inside the magnificent house.

$\triangledown$

2 9

"SKIPPING OUT ON YOUR bill?" Dallas waited until Teresa Jane had opened the trunk of her Lexus before he emerged from the Ocean Tides's lobby.

"I settled up with Susan this morning." She answered as though his question had been genuine.

"I'll help you with that." Dallas carefully laid Teresa Jane's suitcase in the car's spotless trunk.

"I was coming in to say good-bye."

"No, you weren't." Dallas wasn't being accusatory or hurt, just accepting of the fact that she'd planned to head back to New York without wanting to hear him tell her she was wrong for leaving.

Teresa Jane was wearing the suit she'd arrived in, only now the creases weren't quite so sharp. After hanging in an Ocean Tides closet, the fabric had relaxed from its starched salute.

There were lots of things she wanted to tell him, but none she could manage to say.

Dallas took her hand in his. Her fingers were cool with apprehension. "In January, we send out a mailer to everyone who's stayed here over the summer. To get you to send in a deposit we can collect interest on for half a year. When you get one, don't throw it out the window of your penthouse office, okay? Pick a week and come back." He gave her hand a squeeze. "You deserve it."

Her smile was tight, almost painful, but her eyes cast agreement. "I called my father and told him what you found out. I also said I knew

174

he'd come here to see Jud. I asked him why he never told me that, why he pretended to have written Jud off. He denied ever being here. But I know he was lying. My guess is he was trying to force Jud to go back to school, but I'll probably never know for sure. He's been lying to us all our lives. It's never going to stop."

When Dallas moved closer to kiss her, she turned so that his lips touched her cheek; otherwise, it would have made leaving all the harder. "I have to go," she said softly when he pulled away.

"I know."

"I had a fantastic time." The words were there, but her tone of voice was back to New York, as if phoning a client to tell her a stock split had just upped her portfolio ten percent. "It's just that things happen here that shouldn't." It sounded as though she was referring to what the two of them had felt for each other, but then she added sadly, "Something happened to Judson here, Dallas."

Backing slowly away, hands in the pockets of University of Maryland sweat shorts, Dallas shook his head. "What happened to your brother had nothing to do with here. The beach doesn't have that kind of power. But money sure does." Dallas waved. "See you next summer."

He walked into the Ocean Tides lobby, passed Susan without a word, and closed himself into the cubbyhole office where he'd first encountered the whirlwind force that had identified herself as Teresa Jane Fitch.

He waited for her to come in after him, to say she'd changed her mind, that she was staying the rest of the summer, maybe the rest of her life, but it didn't happen.

Tommy raced toward deep left field, made an awkward leap for a fly ball, and robbed the batter of a home run. The catch snared, Tommy smashed into the outfield fence and went sprawling in a dozen directions at once. Flat on the grass, looking as though he'd just burst his spleen, Tommy waited until he was surrounded by concerned teammates before jumping up, taunting, "Ahhhhh-hahhhh! Gotcha!"

They banged him with baseball gloves for acting like an idiot.

"What's the score?" Dallas took a seat beside C.J. on the bench.

"I have no idea." C.J. lay face up; a baseball cap with a sudsy beer logo covered his face to ward off the sun. "All I know is when they tell us to shake hands, the game's over, and I can go home." C.J.'s presence on the bench meant there were only eight players in the field, but he demanded at least one inning's vacation per game.

The rest of the high school kids were all there. Chad, Jason, Ashley, Ricky, Bobby, Billy, Todd — Dallas watched them raise a cloud of dust as they pounded Tommy mercilessly in center field.

The opposing team was getting ticked off with the delay, complaining this happened all the time: that The Brew Crew had more team dissension than most family reunions, but somehow their stranglehold on first place was unsnappable.

The skirmish in center field took five minutes to end, but then Tommy mooned the base runner on second and there was another brawl.

"We get lots of games called on account of darkness," C.J. said from inside his hat.

When Tommy's shorts were back in place, Dallas grabbed a dusty glove off the dugout floor and moved into the vacancy left by C.J.'s absence in right field.

He liked it here. At the beach. With these kids. They were still at the age where the absolute thrill of chasing a screaming line drive was more exciting than negotiating a thousand bucks off the sticker price of a BMW or making sure the house they were having custom built was a hundred square feet bigger than the guy's next door.

The only gloomy aspect was that one day, these kids, too, would meet their own Olivia Miles, their own corrupt stockbroker, someone or something that would change all that. No longer would they be most concerned with trying to stretch a gapper single into a double, or seeing how much action their boogie board could coax out of a small wave.

But that was why Dallas stayed at the beach, to keep at bay all things unavoidable and undeniable. A long time ago Dallas had realized that for him a happy life was stringing together a wandering strand of small pleasures. No lofty goals or cutthroat aspirations to claw the rungs of a corporate ladder. He just wanted to ride the waves.

So when Chad jammed the batter with a slow-arching pitch and a half-checked swing blooped a fat softball into shallow right, Dallas took off with a gallop of aching knees and weak ankles.

In less than two hours, the sun would set and he'd feel empty thinking about Teresa Jane on her way back to New York. He'd picture her alone on busy expressways, fighting traffic, heading unsuspectingly into the snarling jaws of the city.

But that was reality. That was later. Now there was only twenty feet of well-trimmed grass between him and a dropping fly ball he was going to have to dive for.

If you have enjoyed this book and would like to receive details on other Walker mystery titles, please write to:
Mystery Editor
Walker and Company
720 Fifth Avenue
New York, NY 10019